Narrative Structures IN Burmese Folk Tales

Narrative Structures in Burmese Folk Tales

Soe Marlar Lwin

Amherst, New York

Library of Congress Cataloging-in-Publication Data

Lwin, Soe Marlar.
Narrative structures in Burmese folk tales / Soe Marlar Lwin.
p. cm.
Includes bibliographical references and index.
ISBN 978-1-60497-716-5 (alk. paper)
1. Tales—Burma—Structural analysis. 2. Tales—Burma—Classification.
I. Title.

GR309.L87 2010
398.209591—dc22

2010026495

To my Mum and Dad,
with grateful thanks for their love and support

Table of Contents

List of Tables

Preface

This study investigates the narrative structures in the folk tales of Burma (now known as Myanmar), collected and translated into English by Maung Htin Aung. The study first sets out to identify the functional events in these tales as the basic components of a story structure. It then examines how these events are linked into various plot structures in different types of tales. The study also attempts to relate the form (narrative structure) of a folk tale to its function (social purpose) and field (narrative content) by comparing two structural patterns identified in the analysis of Burmese folk tales with those proposed by other studies of folk tales from different cultures. The possibilities of using a structural analysis of folk tales as a means of understanding not only the commonalities but also the uniqueness in structural patterns, narrative contents, and social purposes of folk tales from different cultures are also explored in this study.

First, for the analysis of functional events, Propp's (1968) concept of function is adapted. The study classifies these functional events identified in Burmese folk tales into various models, according to the similarities in structural patterns. For the examination of temporal and/or causal relations between events forming the storyline of a tale, the study applies the narrative dimension of linearity, as proposed by Ochs and Capps (2001).

The results from the analysis show that, although functional events serve as the basic constituents in a tale, their combination sequences may vary, creating different structural patterns. Functional events in the narrative structures of different types of tales are found to be interconnected in different ways. Although the sequence of functional events in a tale may not be identical to that of the other, as is claimed in Propp's study, the linear and coherent storyline for a well-organised narrative structure can still be explained with Ochs and Capps' (2001) concept of sequential meaning. The analysis of Burmese folk tales uncovers the various ways in which functional events of a folk tale are linked logically in agreement with the prevailing causality of the storyline. In a few cases, some deviations from these familiar trajectories have been observed, causing such special effects as humour.

A comparison between the two prominent structural patterns identified in the analysis of Burmese folk tales and those discussed in earlier and recent studies of folk tales from other cultures (e.g., Korean) shows that despite certain culture-specific narrative contents, tales with similar social purposes (e.g., a didactic moral purpose) exhibit similar structural patterns. This finding suggests that certain structural patterns are used commonly (if not universally) by various cultures for the similar social purpose of storytelling. At the same time, the finding also implies that although different cultures may share the same structural pattern, the narrative contents of a tale (e.g., elements taking up the narrative roles) remain culture specific. This has pointed to several interesting issues, such as the (im)possibilities of finding a universal grammar of folk tales and the viability of claims about commonalities among folk tales from adjacent countries, given that adjacent countries are most likely to have influenced each other's culture.

This study is presented in seven chapters. Chapter 1 provides some background information about Burma and its folk tales analysed in this study. Chapter 2 reviews relevant literature on studies of narrative and events as its fundamental requirement. The chapter also looks at the structural analyses of folk tales performed in the earlier studies and comments on the different approaches to an analysis of narrative structures. The pivotal issues and some justifications are also explained. Chapter 3 outlines the research methodology used in this study for the analysis of Burmese folk tales. It details the procedures of the analysis and offers a sample analysis of a tale using the proposed frameworks.

Chapter 4 presents the analysis and findings from all 27 tales included in the collection. All the functional events identified in these tales are recorded before they are classified into various structural patterns. Tales with different models in the storyline, and the linkage in each model, are illustrated in detail with some sample analyses. Chapter 5 moves on to discuss the findings from the analysis, with a focus on such notions as functions, moves, connectives, linearity, and well-organised storylines in the narrative structures of folk tales. Attempts are then made in chapter 6 to discover the relationships between the narrative structure (form), social purpose (function), and narrative content (field) of a tale by comparing two structural patterns commonly found in Burmese folk tales with those found in other studies of tales from different cultures. Finally, chapter 7 outlines the conclusions drawn from the present study and offers some recommendations for those who may find this study and the issues it has uncovered interesting to explore further.

ACKNOWLEDGMENTS

I am indebted to Maung Htin Aung (Dr Htin Aung) for his invaluable collections and translation of Burmese folk tales. His works on Burmese culture have been an inspiration for this study of narrative structures in Burmese folk tales. I would like to thank Sterling Publishers, Oxford University Press (India), and Oxford University Press (U.K.) for their permissions to use these tales in my study.

I am also thankful to A/P Ismail Talib for his guidance, encouragement, and help throughout the length of my studies at the National University of Singapore. My research interests in narrative structures, folk tales, and oral storytelling have grown vastly under his valuable supervision. My thanks also go to the reviewers of this book for their insightful comments and suggestions.

This book would not have been possible without the help and support from Dr Paul Richardson of Cambria Press. I am most thankful to him for his kind help, understanding, and encouragement throughout this project. Thanks also to the staff of Cambria Press who deserves a commendation for their resourcefulness and efficiency, especially the director, Ms Toni Tan.

Narrative Structures in Burmese Folk Tales

Chapter 1

Introduction

Burmese folk tales have been preserved as part of a long folk tradition reflecting Burmese humour, romance, and wisdom. Before writing systems were developed, Burmese folk tales were handed down orally from generation to generation. Some of them have been collected and translated into English in order to further the appreciation of Burmese culture by English-speaking readers.

Burma, now officially known as the Union of Myanmar, is situated in Southeast Asia, sharing its border with China, Laos, Thailand, Bangladesh, India, and the Bay of Bengal. Due to border contact, immigration, or invasion in the early history of the nation, Burmese culture has been influenced by the cultures of these neighbouring countries. This influence is manifested in various aspects—such as language, literature, cuisine, religion, and arts. In addition, as a country comprising many distinct ethnic groups, Burmese culture is also rich with its own local elements. Besides the Bamar (Burman), which make up more than 60% of the population, the other major ethnic groups include the Kachin, the Kayah, the Karen, the Chin, the Mon, the Rakhine, and the Shan.

With an aim to investigate and describe some features of narrative structures in Burmese folk tales, this study will examine the 27 tales collected and translated into English by Maung Htin Aung, a major figure in the literature on Burmese folk tales. The titles of all 27 folk tales analysed in this study are listed in appendix A. The collection of tales includes those of the Bamar, Burma's predominant tribe, as well as those of other ethnic groups. In this first chapter, the background information of the study and some important issues generally related to studies of folk tales will be discussed.

1.1. FOLK TALES

Folk tales in general are part of folk literature, which is more widely referred to as folklore. They can be classified as one of the categories of folk storytelling. Many folklorists have labelled myths, legends, and folk tales as major narrative genres in folklore, 'according to how the narrative is received by the community' (Swales, 1990, p. 35). Myths are stories that are considered sacred, legends are more secular recounting of actual events, and folk tales are narrative regarded as fiction (Eugenio, 1995). Simply put, a folk tale is a traditional story that has been passed on by word of mouth before writing systems were developed.

Various studies have been conducted on folk tales, reflecting the wide-ranging and multidisciplinary interest in them. In addition to cultural-historical, philological-literary, and comparative research, modern folklore has increasingly employed sociological, psychological, pedagogic, functional, and structural approaches (Röhrich, 1991). Folklorists have analysed and categorised tales from various regions in terms of the subject, title, motif, and ethnic or geographical area (e.g., MacDonald, 1982). The telling of folk tales has also been one of the activities that 'provide[s] the descriptive linguist and the philologist with texts for phonetic, lexical and syntactical analysis and comparison' (Abbott & Khin, 2000, p. 5).

Because these tales have been originally disseminated verbally, some modification is inevitable. Martin (1986) has mentioned that writing and printing may have affected 'the production of stories "told" by an author who is not present to a solitary reader' (p. 33). However, according to Rimmon-Kenan (1983), 'story, as the narrated events and participants abstracted from the text, can be claimed as transferable from medium to medium, from language to language, and within the same language' (p. 6). Jason (1977) also asserted that 'the narrative can be translated into another language and even into another medium of communication...and still keep its structure' (p. 99). Thus, the focus of the present study will be on the fundamental events forming the story structure of some Burmese folk tales written in English, which can be claimed to have survived paraphrase or translation.

The tales selected for the present study were collected and translated into English by Maung Htin Aung, who has been recognised for producing the first ever published collection of Burmese tales in English. Maung's works in English on the tales of Burma include: *Burmese Folk-Tales* (1948), *Burmese Law Tales* (1962), *Burmese Monk's Tales* (1966), and *Folk Tales of Burma* (1976). The introduction to his first published collection, *Burmese Folk-Tales* (1948), stated that tales of this kind were told in Burma up to about the time of the First World War, had become 'half-forgotten' by the end of the Second World War, and were collected between 1933 and 1937. A particular volume, *Folk Tales of Burma*,[1] published by Sterling Publishers, was chosen for the present study because it is part of the series Folk Tales of the World.

The first in-depth overview of Burmese folk-tale studies was recently undertaken by Abbott and Khin (2000). With comments and analyses on plots and cross-cultural motifs, they offered a broad, functional classification of Burmese folk tales. Their classification of tales is based on two factors: *function* (the social purpose of folklore) and *field* (narrative motif or the content). *Form* or structure, another major factor for classification in a genre (Swales, 1990), was not used as a criterion in their study.

With disapproving comments on the little success of the structural approaches to the folk tale, Abbott and Khin (2000) recommended the analysis of narrative structures in Burmese folk tales by further research. Some possible approaches to an understanding of the delivery and structure of folk tales were also suggested, such as 'the application of recent works on genre analysis by linguists and language educators', 'the application of a "story schema"', or 'the sociolinguistic analysis of speech acts' (Abbott & Khin, 2000, pp. 44–45). The present study will, therefore, examine narrative structures in Burmese folk tales, an area of research that has remained to be explored.

CHAPTER 2

NARRATIVE AND ITS STRUCTURES

In this chapter, some key terms and concepts pertinent to studies of narrative and its structure—such as events, plots, and story logic—will be discussed. The pivotal issues that the present study aims to address in the following chapters will also be outlined and some justification will be provided.

2.1. NARRATIVE, EVENTS, AND PLOTS

Narrative is a term that is difficult to define in both literary theory and discourse analysis. Toolan (1998) claimed that '[n] early everyone has a strong sense of what is a narrative and what is not a narrative, but failsafe definitions are hard to come by' (p. 136). With regard to problems with definitions on narrative,

Talib (2002) pointed out that in most of the attempts to define narrative, the reuse of such words as *narrative* and *narration* in explaining the concept does not really give any new information on the term and makes the definitions circular. For example, Chatman (1978) defined narrative as a structure that comprises narrative statements. Rimmon-Kenan (1983) defined narrative fiction as the narration of a succession of fictional events. Bal (1985) defined narrative as a corpus that should consist of all narrative texts and only those texts that are narrative.

What is noteworthy in all these attempts to define narrative is a certain degree of agreement among them on its dualistic nature; in other words, narrative comprises a *what* (narrative content, such as events, actors, time, and location) and a *way* (how the narrative is told) (Talib, 2004, 1.2). Following the Russian Formalists and French Structuralists, narrative has been described by Chatman (1978) as having a binary structure: *story* (the formal content element) and *discourse* (the formal expression element). It was later split into three levels by Rimmon-Kenan (1983) as *story*, *text*, and *narration*, and by Bal (1985) as *fabula*, *story*, and *text*.

In spite of some disparity in their use of the terms, the first term in either the two- or three-level descriptions, *story* or *fabula*, can be understood as 'a basic description of the fundamental events of a story' and can be regarded as the level with 'the possibility of "total transfer" from one medium to another' (Toolan, 1988, p. 9). Conversely, the second term roughly refers to the textual realisation of the story, and denotes the 'varying manner of presentation of the basic story' (Toolan, 1988, 2001, p. 10).

Subsequently, a minimalist definition of narrative, that is, 'a perceived sequence of non-randomly connected events' (p. 7) has been provided by Toolan (1988). According to Toolan (1998),

> A narrative…is at minimum a text (or text-like artistic production) in which the reader or addressee perceives a significant change. In a narrative,…one state of affairs is displaced by a different state of affairs, and this latter state is, ideally, not merely temporally but causally related to the former state. (p. 136)

The recognition of narrative as a sequence of events can be inferred from the aforementioned minimal view on narrative. It can be concluded that for a discussion of narrative and its structure, events (particularly a sequence of events) are often regarded as an important characteristic and a significant narratological[2] concept. To quote Bal (1985), an 'event is the transition from one state to another state' (p. 13). In her three-level description of narrative (*fabula*, *story*, *text*), *fabula* is a series of logically and chronologically related events caused or experienced by actors. It is regarded as the deep or abstract structure of the text. The crucial role of events in a narrative structure was also discussed by Rimmon-Kenan (1983):

> Structural descriptions of narrative show how events combine to create micro-sequences which in turn combine to form macro-sequences which jointly create the complete story. (p. 15)

Toolan (1988) then clearly asserted that 'an event, bringing a change of state, is the most fundamental requirement in narrative' (p. 90). Indeed, the temporal sequencing of two or more events has been considered by many to be a hallmark of narrative (Ochs & Capps, 2001). However, as has been pointed out by Leitch (1986) and also by Toolan (1988), a random set of events cannot be a story. An analysis of the narrative structures will thus devote considerable attention to plot structure—the organisation of events in the plot or the relationship that connects one event to the other.

It is important to note that although most minimalist definitions of a narrative cover the two generally accepted criteria of sequentiality (temporal succession) and causality (either explicit or implicit) between events, the concept of events forming a narrative is better understood only when it is discussed in connection with its related concept (i.e., the plot, or the ways in which events are represented, or 'the order in which events are recounted' [Abbott, 2002, p. 16]).

An analysis of narrative structure from this perspective can help us realise that in addition to a single closed storyline of beginning, middle, and end, the structures of different types of narrative may show the varying degree of connectedness, non-randomness, and sequentiality of events in a plot. Accordingly, a narrative genre can be examined as a certain combination of functional events; the differences between the genres of narrative can be understood as partly the result of the different possible combinations of event sequences (Güttgemanns, 1977).

For example, the differences in narrative structures between literary genres of narrative and personal narrative have been discussed by Ochs and Capps (2001). They showed how the storylines in informal conversations are open-ended, incomplete, or unresolved, whereas interview narratives may first yield a tidy story that subsequently disintegrates. 'The narrative structures of these types of narrative may or may not encompass a beginning, middle, and end since it depends on how interlocutors attempt to craft the plot' (Ochs & Capps, 2001, p. 57). Swales (1990) also claimed that

> specific types of narrative diverge from the pre-generic norm and thus begin to acquire genre status. Thus in news stories the temporal succession is disturbed by putting 'the freshest on the top'...Jokes have temporal

> sequences, agent orientation and plot, but the resolution of the plot is specific: the moment of resolution needs to be overtly signaled...whilst the manner of resolution needs to be unpredictable. (p. 61)

Conversely, the structure of a simple tale (such as a folk tale) is expected to follow an overarching storyline with proper beginning, middle, and end. It is also a general rule that the narrative sequence in the folk storytelling coincides with the sequence of actions being described. However, the entire sense of the folk tale is not restricted to 'Once upon a time' and 'They lived happily ever after' (Oring, 1986, p. 134). An analysis of narrative structures in folk tales needs to identify the fundamental events by which the narrative is 'driven' into a well-organised storyline, as well as to investigate whether these events can be claimed as identical for all types of tales, and how they are linked into familiar trajectories.

2.2. Events and Story Logic

Before moving on to review studies of narrative structures in folk tales, it is important to point out that events in some narrative texts (e.g., fantastic, absurd, or experimental) may not correspond with the logic of reality, as these texts are characterised by their denial or distortion of such logic. In such cases, the readers' powerful tendency to search for a logical line becomes an answer to the question of how the logic of events can be implied or how the events are put together to form a plot. Bal (1985) contended that

> if necessary, they [readers] introduce such a line themselves. No matter how absurd, tangled, or unreal a text may be, readers will tend to regard what they consider 'normal' as a criterion by which they can give meaning to the text. (p. 12)

Thus, it is important to understand the logic of events in a broader sense, in other words, as a course of events that is experienced by the reader as natural and in accordance with the world.

Chatman (1978) also suggested contingency as one of the organising principles for events, besides sequence and causality. He claimed that what is important to a general theory of narrative is not the precise linguistic manifestation but rather the story logic. Chatman (1978) defined contingency in a stricter philosophical sense of 'depending for its existence, occurrence, character etc. on something not yet certain' (p. 47). Chatman's proposal on the relationship of events and their sequences to story logic has been further investigated by Herman (2002) with his exploration on verb types and event structures in storyworld (re)construction. Herman distinguished event types (activities, achievement, accomplishment, and states) based on the semantic implications of verbs. He regarded different event types realised by the semantic implications of verbs as semantic resources the narrator can resort to in cuing recipients to model certain kinds of storyworlds. From this perspective, Herman argued that different narrative modes set distinct preference-rule systems of event types into play.

A preference-based typology of event types in different narrative genres is also examined in Herman's study. The study proposed, for example, that the preference ranking of event types for an epic will be 'Accomplishments > achievements > activities > states' while that of a ghost story will be 'Activities > states > accomplishments > achievements' (Herman, 2002, p. 37). He also noted that the parameter for classifying event types is not their goal directedness, but rather the temporal extension and definiteness in the (re)construction of the storyworld. Such classification, Herman claimed, is able to capture not only the *punctual* events (i.e., events creating 'clear-cut transitions between narrative states') but also *durative* events (i.e., '[e]vents with temporal extension blurring the distinction between active and stative propositions') (Herman, 2002, p. 32).

From this perspective, the concept of events goes beyond understanding them as actions. Instead, actions are suggested as a special type of events among others, and stories are described as an interweavement of various event types. Herman (2002) asserted that understanding events as actions 'does not provide a sufficiently fine-grained account of states, events, actions, and how they are related to one another' (p. 38). Because different narrative genres have created different patterns of propositions, events can be fully understood as a resource for microdesigning narratives only by relating them to the story logic.

2.3. Structural Analysis of Folk Tales

There has been extensive literature on narrative because it has been a topic of sustaining interest to linguists and literary critics (Toolan, 1988). It must also be admitted that the study of a storyline over time and across distance is not a new pursuit. One of the most famous works on the structural analysis of folk tales was completed by the Russian scholar Vladimir Propp on Russian fairy tales. It is often claimed that the structural or morphological study of folk tales and mythology begins with Propp.

Propp's *Morphology of the Folktale*, published in Russian in 1928, was translated into English in 1958 and published in a revised edition in 1968. His study included 115 of the Russian fairy tales collected by Alexander Afanas'ev. Propp (1968) defined *morphology* as 'a description of the tale according to its component parts and the relationship of these components to each other and to the whole' (p.19).

Propp's (1968) structural analysis was based on *function* or *functional event*, which was defined as '*what* a tale's dramatis personae do' (p. 20). He described tales as consisting of, first, narrative actions, which he proved to be constant, and, second, narrative roles, which are variable. He claimed that 'all tales, however different they were as to their dramatis personae and their plot, had an identical sequence of functions, and the same basic structure' (Propp, 1975, p. 164).

In his analysis, Propp listed every functional event that emerged in the tales selected for his study, and proposed a set of 31 functional events, which, he claimed, appeared in the same order. These functional events have been grouped into four sequences: 'Introductory sequence, Body of the story, Donor sequence, and Protagonist's return' (Rouheir-Willoughby, para. 1, 2, 3, 4). Propp's (1968) study proved the following four hypotheses, in relation to the corpus of Russian fairy tales that he studied:

1. Functions of characters serve as stable, constant elements in a tale, independent of how and by whom they are fulfilled. They constitute the fundamental components of a tale.
2. The number of functions known to the fairy tale is limited.
3. The sequence of functions is always identical.
4. All fairy tales are of one type in regard to their structure. (pp. 21–23)

Following Propp, Dundes (1965, 1971) studied the structures of folk tales from various cultures. In applying Propp's morphological framework to American Indian folk tales, Dundes (1965) replaced *function* with *motifeme*, and studied their structural typology. Folk tales have been defined as a sequence of motifemes.

A much more common motifeme sequence has been described as: 'Interdiction, Violation, Consequence, and an Attempted Escape from the Consequence' (Dundes, 1965, p. 209).

Although Dundes' study did not discuss all the existing motifeme patterns, his few illustrative patterns supported the thesis that American Indian folk tales are structured. Moreover, the significance and use of structural analyses on folk tales was highlighted as a new technique of gaining insight into the cultural determination of content. Analysis of structures was recommended for making typological statements, for predicting an acculturation situation, and for making cross-genre comparison such as the folk tale and superstition. Structural analysis of folklore of different geographical areas was also suggested in order to reveal whether certain structural patterns are universal (Dundes, 1965).

With the designation of a minimal unit of analysis—the *function* for Propp and the *motifeme* for Dundes—the identification of structural patterns becomes easier, and presents important theoretical implications for both folk-tale scholarship and the study of narrative structures in general. However, Georges (1970) pointed out that these studies fail to account for the existence and operations of the patterns or, in other words, how the patterns come into existence or how they are generated. Following the procedure used in generative-transformational grammar, Georges (1970) argued that

> folktales, like grammatical sentences in any given language, are generated systematically. Through a series of ordered operations, narrative structures containing a finite number of elements arranged in a fixed sequence are generated. (p. 6)

Georges (1970) defined a folk tale as a traditional narrative composed of a *Move* and a *Countermove*, which consist of *Initial*

Motifemic Cluster and *Final Motifemic Cluster*, respectively. His operational procedure explained how each cluster consists of elements such as Lack, Task, Interdiction, Violation, Deceit, and Consequence. Narrative structures identified in his study are proposed to operate in the following patterns:

1. Task + Task Accomplished
2. Interdiction + Violation + Consequence + Attempted Escape
3. Interdiction + Violation + Consequence
4. Lack + Deceit + Deception + Consequence
5. Deceit + Deception + Consequence (Georges, 1970, p.10)

Georges' (1970) study put forth the implication that the basic narrative structure is generated before the content is ordered. It can be criticised as a transformational grammar, which has been pressed into service by the folklorist on material that is quite resistant to it. However, Georges' (1970) study should be acknowledged for its attempt to explain not only the basic patterns, which can exist as independent tales, but also the complexity in the narrative structure of folk tales. The complexity is the result of either the concatenation (i.e., chaining together) of these sequences or through a process of embedding (i.e., inserting one sequential pattern between narrative elements of another). It also laid the foundation, in spite of its flaws, for a consideration of the process involved in folk-tale creation and re-creation.

2.4. Different Approaches to an Analysis of Narrative Structures

Sceptics on structuralism commented that the structural analysis of narrative is suitable only for the simplest form of narrative, like folk tales (Genette, 1980). However, with the growing interest in narrative as a social and psychological phenomenon, rather than solely as a formal literary or historical genre, attempts to discover basic story structures have extended into studies on structural principles in other forms of narrative.

One such well-known study was conducted by Labov and Waletzky (1967). Unlike Propp, they proposed, first, that the clause is the smallest unit of linguistic expression that defines the functions of narrative. Second, they claimed that 'any sequence of clauses which contains at least one temporal juncture' is a minimum structure that provides a unit of analysis (Labov & Waletzky, 1967, p. 28). They presented an analytical framework for the analysis of oral versions of personal experience in English. A fully formed oral narrative is shown to have a six-part structure as follows:

1. Abstract: What was the story about?
2. Orientation: Who, when, what, where?
3. Complication action: Then what happened?
4. Evaluation: So what?
5. Result or resolution: What finally happened?
6. Coda: The sealing off of a narrative, which signals that the narrative is finished.

Labov (1972) contended that this sequencing can be taken as the 'default' or simplest format. The study also asserted that in simpler oral narratives, and in fables and fairy tales, the six elements listed tend to occur, and it will be in the given order if they do occur. His study has been recognised as providing the basis for the analysis of the narrative structure in spoken discourse. However, it has been criticised as having left out the context of the telling of the story (Lepper, 2000). Although the study is based on the oral versions of personal experience, which should be socially situated, the focus is on the relationship of the parts of the narrative to each other, rather than on that of the producer to the recipient of the story.

Another study, which can be characterised as being concerned with structural principles in narrative, was conducted by Harvey Sacks. Based on his analysis of stories in conversations, Sacks (1992) claimed that storytelling is ubiquitous in naturally occurring interaction and that the default organisation in narratives is more than a matter of narrative technique or of discourse organisation. Sacks' analysis of stories in conversations pointed out the orderly sequences of storytelling, as governed by embedded rules of production and turn-taking in the situated context of the telling. The studies of narrative structures in a context by Labov and Sacks provide the basis for the investigation of storytelling as an extensive social phenomenon.

Such an analysis of sequential compositional structure is just one type of structural analysis (Dundes, 1971; Jason & Segal, 1977). The structure of the texture of a narrative can also be appropriately examined. For example, unlike the studies that investigate a distinct story structure, Hasan (1996) and Hoey (2001) focused on the other layer of narrative—discourse, or the concrete level of textual realisation. Taking a generic approach, Hasan (1996) studied the nursery tale as a genre. Hasan's (1996) Generic Structure Potential (GSP) illustrates the typical sequence of the major narrative elements in nursery tale as follows:

[(<Placement>)Initiating Event^]Sequent Event^Final Event[^(Finale)*(Moral)] (p. 54)

The elements in round brackets are considered as optional while those not in round brackets are regarded as obligatory. The angle brackets enclose elements that have lexicogrammatical realisation which may be included or interspersed with lexico-grammatical realisation of some other elements. The raised dot * between elements refers to their reversibility, while the carat sign indicates relative fixity. Square brackets indicate that the two elements can precede one another, and curved arrow symbolises the possibility of iteration for that element. Hasan (1996) used the GSP framework in examining the structure of nursery tales in order to display their common entities, and to put forth a better definition of a nursery tale among other categories of narratives. The recognition of optionality in her study, both for the elements and for their order vis-à-vis each other, builds in the possibility of variation in the structure of the texture of a narrative.

Conversely, Hoey (2001) proposed another way of understanding narrative structure, which is in terms of narrative matrices. A narrative matrix is formed with participants in the horizontal parameter, and time bands in the vertical parameter. Any telling of a happening is seen as tracing a path through the matrix. Distinguishing the structure of a happening from the structure of a telling of that happening, his study illustrates matrix analyses of some narrative texts such as *Cinderella, Goldilocks and the Three Bears*, and *Aesop* stories. Time-sequence-oriented narrative matrices are observed by answering the iterative question 'What happened next?' which is usually interspersed with questions relating to the description of the scene or the thoughts of the characters (Hoey, 2001). Hasan's (1996) and Hoey's (2001) studies discussed the techniques that authors take in their varying manner of presentation of the basic story.

Alternatively, in their study of personal narratives, Ochs and Capps (2001) discussed the differences between telling a story *to* another and telling a story *with* another. Comparing the plot structures of literary and oral narratives, they pointed out that in a written narrative the opening, middle, and end have already been established, leading to an overwhelming proclivity 'to construct an overarching storyline that ties events together in a seamless explanatory framework' (Ochs & Capps, 2001, p. 4).

Instead of finding out narrative theories that are usually self-contained, they took what they called a *dimensional* approach to narrative. They believed that narrative as genre and activity can be fruitfully examined in terms of a set of dimensions that a narrative displays to differing degrees and in different ways. The five narrative dimensions proposed in their study are outlined in table 1. The dimension of *tellership* refers to the extent and kind of involvement of partners. This dimension assesses how the relatively high involvement of partners or co-telling of a story can affirm or challenge the prevailing storyline. *Tellability* is the extent to which a narrative conveys a sequence of reportable events and makes a point in a rhetorically effective manner. It is also related to the significance of events for particular interlocutors. *Embeddedness* is the degree and kind of integration with surrounding discourse, such as narrative embeddedness in prayers, explanation, and other speech activities. *Linearity* is the extent to which narratives depict events as transpiring in a single, closed, temporal, and causal path or, alternatively, in diverse, open, uncertain paths. *Moral stance* is the narrative perspective assumed by tellers and protagonists (Ochs & Capps, 2001, pp. 33–54).

Each narrative dimension establishes a range of possibilities, which can be used to analyse how the telling of a narrative is shaped, and how events are structured through narrative form. In other words, their study brought different aspects of narrative—such as storyline, textual realisation, and context—to light. Recognising the prosaic as well as artistic realisations of narrative, they proposed the framework that can be applied to

Table 1. Narrative dimensions and possibilities.

Dimensions	Possibilities		
Tellership	One active teller	→	Multiple active co-tellers
Tellability	High	→	Low
Embeddedness	Detached	→	Embeddedness
Linearity	Closed temporal and causal order	→	Open temporal and causal order
Moral stance	Certain, constant	→	Uncertain, fluid

Source. Ochs & Capps, 2001, p. 20.

measure the narrative proclivities of both conversational narrative and literary genres of narrative.

The review of earlier studies of narrative structures can be summarised as follows. On the one hand, the studies by Propp (1968), Dundes (1965), and Georges (1970) showed various methods of identifying a story structure in folk tales. The studies by Hasan (1996) and Hoey (2001), on the other hand, took a generic approach and focused on the level of discourse or textual realisation of the story. Labov (1972), Sacks (1992), and Ochs and Capps (2001) studied the structural framework of oral narratives from sociolinguistic perspectives. Toolan (1988), alternatively, proposed the grammaticalisation of core narrative clauses as a method of highlighting basic story structure. His method can be regarded as a stylistic approach to narrative, which is a counterpart to the structural analysis of narrative (Lüthi, 1982).

From the review of literature, a structural analysis of narrative can be performed in relation to different aspects, such as text (story structure), texture (concrete level of textual realisation), and context (actual social situation of narrative). Dundes (1971) has suggested that 'the structures of texture, text, and context may be parallel or otherwise meaningfully interrelated' (p. 173).

Among all these different aspects, the present study chooses the aspect of story structure. It aims to identify the functional events forming the storylines in some Burmese folk tales and their relation in various models of the basic story structure. With the focus of the study on the story, as extracted from the text, it is hoped that the basic story structures investigated in the present study will be able to represent an interpretative or evaluative framework for future research in the two other aspects of texture and context.

2.5. Pivotal Issues and Some Justifications

With an aim to investigate the narrative structures in Burmese folk tales, the study will first examine how functional events are linked into plot structures in different types of tales. An analysis of tales will be done to address the following questions:

1. What are the functional events that constitute different types of Burmese folk tales?
2. How can they be specified into the minimum number of functional events making up various structural patterns?
3. How are they linked into highly linear plot structures?
4. Are there any systematic deviations from familiar trajectories, and what effects do these deviations have on the storyline of a tale?

Following the examination of narrative structures in a collection of tales, the study will then explore the possibilities of relating the narrative structure (form) with the social purpose (function) and the story content (field) of a folk tale. For this purpose, the study will use the two most striking features identified in the analysis of narrative structures in Burmese folk tales and compare them with tales from other cultures as examples. Through an illustration of the relationship between the narrative form, function, and field of tales from two cultures, the study hopes to propose a structural analysis of folk tales as a means of gaining insight into the cultural determination of the narrative motif and the social purpose of storytelling.

Although the study of a storyline in folk tales is not a newfound area of research, any systematic differences in the plot structures of different types of Burmese folk tales may still prove to be thought provoking. Propp's (1968) study, which has been recognised as a groundbreaking work in the analysis of narrative structure, is corpus specific (i.e., limited to Russian fairy tales). Zipes (2000) has pointed out that the fairy tale is only one type of literary appropriation of a particular oral storytelling tradition related to the oral wonder tales. Dundes (1980) has also commented that fairy stories and other folk tales can change in both form and field not only over time but also across ethnic boundaries. Thus, with the analysis of the narrative structures in different types of Burmese folk tales, the present study intends to propose story structure as a possible criterion in the categorisation of different types of tales in a culture, and probably also of tales across different cultures.

As noted earlier, Propp (1968) claimed that the number of functional events in Russian fairy tales is limited to 31, and that the sequence of these functional events is fixed. This does not imply that all 31 possible functional events necessarily occur in any one given tale. The only one absolutely necessary functional event, he claimed, is 'villainy (A) or a lack (a)' (Propp, 1968, p. 92). This definition should be broadened by specifying the minimum number of functional events and the minimum number of connecting links that are necessary to constitute a folk tale. It has been suggested by Ochs and Capps (2001) that linearity as a narrative dimension can be measured in a range of degrees and displayed in a variety of ways. Hence, the present study hopes to advance Propp's model with the findings on how the events can be interlocked with each other linearly in a plot structure, which may or may not comprise identical functional events and combination sequences.

While examining how the events are linked into familiar trajectories, the study will also take note of any deviation from them and will explore what effect such deviation has on the storyline of a tale. With this, the present study will argue that, instead of looking for a single pattern in plots that may be different across different types of tales, an analysis of narrative structures should investigate various possible temporal and/or causal linkage with which events are bound together into well-organised storylines.

The study may prove that Burmese folk tales follow similar patterns, which conform to patterns common elsewhere. Systematic, recurrent aspects of stories do not lead to mere resemblance. A typical storyline can be proposed as a system capable of tracing any structural likeness, especially in folk tales of adjacent nations. The potential analogy of folk-tale structures may add on the possibility of finding a universal model capable of generating narratives in this genre.

CHAPTER 3

METHODOLOGY

The 27 tales in the collection selected for the study have been divided into two parts by the collector:

1. Tales 1 to 17—*Folk Tales of the Plains*, which are folk tales of Burma's major ethnic group, the Bamar (Burman), and
2. Tales 18 to 27—*Folk Tales of the Hills*, which are folk tales of other ethnic groups of Burma.

Following their thematic resemblance, the collector again divided the *Folk Tales of the Plains* into 'Animal Tales, Wonder Tales, Humour Tales, Proverbial Tales, Ghost Tales, and Law Tales' (Maung, 1976, pp. 5–6). For the analysis of narrative structures in these tales, Propp's (1968) concept of functional events, and Ochs and Capps' (2001) narrative dimension of linearity will be used as the theoretical frameworks of the present study.

3.1. IDENTIFYING FUNCTIONAL EVENTS

Given that an event, bringing a change of state, is the most fundamental requirement in narrative, labelling of events and states in terms of Propp's functional events is one of the methods to analyse the basic story structure (Toolan, 1988). As discussed earlier, Propp (1968) claimed that functional events, as an act of a character defined from the point of view of its significance for the course of the action, can be extracted as basic components of the tale. Following Propp's definition of functional events, the first phase of analysis will be the extraction of all the functional events making up these selected tales.

To be able to extract the functional events from the tales, it is necessary to explain the distribution of narrative roles by the characters in each tale. The 31 functional events proposed in Propp's study are distributed among seven leading dramatis personae. These leading narrative roles can be defined as follows (Propp, 1968, pp. 79–80):

- the villain, who struggles with the Protagonist
- the donor, who prepares and/or provides Protagonist with the magical agent
- the helper, who assists, rescues, solves and/or transfigures the Protagonist
- the Princess, a sought-for-person (and/or her father), who exists as a goal and often recognises and marries Protagonist and/or punishes villain

- the dispatcher, who sends the Protagonist off
- the Hero, who departs on a search (seeker-Protagonist), reacts to the donor, and weds at end
- the false hero (or antihero or usurper), who claims to be the Protagonist, often seeking and reacting like a real Protagonist

The classifications of some of these narrative roles have to be broadened for the present study so that they can be applied to the narrative roles taken by various characters in different types of tales, including the animal tales. A major character carrying out the functional events in the plot will broadly be identified as the Protagonist, instead of the Hero or the Princess. Moreover, it will be more appropriate to define the two protagonists in some tales as *Protagonist A* versus *Protagonist B*, rather than Hero versus Villain, when they are competing on equal terms. Because a tale can have more than one major character, they will be identified as Protagonist A, B, C, etc., as they take the role of major characters for functional events in the tale. Following the classification of characters in each tale to the appropriate narrative roles, the functional events constituting a storyline will be identified.

3.1.1. A Sample Analysis of Functional Events

Tale 3: 'Why the Snail's Muscles Never Ache?' [*sic*]

Distribution of characters to narrative roles:

Protagonist A: The Snail
Protagonist B: The Horse
Helper: Cousin Snails

'Why the Snail's Muscles Never Ache?'[3]	Events
The Horse passed the Snail on the road, and in a contemptuous tone shouted, 'The slow must always give way to the swift'. The Snail replied with dignity, 'We Snails run swiftly only in a race'. The Horse laughed loudly at this, and the Snail challenged him to a race to run the next morning. The Horse accepted the challenge.	1. Lack or insufficiency in one of the Protagonists. (Lack in Protagonist A.)
The Snail summoned all his cousin-snails to him. 'Look here, you fellows', said he, 'Horseflesh is medicinal; it cures paining limbs and aching muscles. Do you want to have some?' All the cousin-snails replied that they wouldn't mind a little bit of horseflesh. 'All right', said the Snail, 'Now listen carefully to my instructions'. He then told them to line the road for many miles, and instructed that between each cousin-snail the distance was to be exactly one furlong. The Snail went to sleep after that, and the cousin-snails walked to their respective stations along the road. As they walked so slowly, it took them the whole day and night to be ready for the race. The next morning the Horse came to the Snail and asked with due sarcasm, 'Are you ready, Master Runner?'	2. Protagonist A meets Helper.
The Snail replied that he was ready and laid down the conditions for the race; the runners should run on and on along the road until one was left behind, and at every furlong the runners should call out to each other to signify that neither had fallen behind. The Horse agreed, and the race started. The Horse ran swiftly, but the Snail walked at a leisurely pace.	3. Protagonist A attempts to harm Protagonist B with trickery. 4. Protagonist B submits to Protagonist A's trickery.
At the first furlong, the Horse shouted, 'Are you still in the race, Master Runner?'	5. Protagonist B complies with deceitful persuasion.

(*continued on next page*)

(continued)

'Why the Snail's Muscles Never Ache?'[3]	Events
'Of course I am', said a cousin-snail, and the Horse was really surprised. He stopped and looked round carefully, and saw the cousin-snail walking sedately by his side. The Horse thought that the cousin-snail was the Snail, and said, 'I will outstrip you all right at the next furlong'. But at the next furlong, there was a cousin-snail ready to pretend that he was the Snail. At last, the Horse fell down dead as a result of too much running.	6. The victory of Protagonist A and the fall of Protagonist B.
The Snail and the cousin-snails later ate up the dead body of the Horse. And up to this day, painful limbs and aching muscles are unknown to the snails.	

3.2. Identifying Different Structural Patterns

The next phase of analysis will be the arrangement of functional events identified in all the selected tales into groups so as to identify the different structural patterns for different types of tales. Tales that comprise similar functional events will be classified as belonging to one type. A tale may comprise only one elementary sequence of functional events, but some of them can comprise more than one, each with its own structural pattern. Therefore, for an illustration of different models and an investigation of the linkage between events in each model, functional events alone become insufficient. The notions of *move* by Propp (1968) and *connectives* by Jason (1977) have to be considered.

Move is a label introduced by Propp (1968) for a series of functional events. Propp explained that a new villainous act creates a new 'move' (Propp, 1968, p. 59). Distinguishing moves in each tale, Propp's analysis showed how a single tale comprises a series of moves. Based on Propp's (1968) notion of move, Jason (1977) introduced an additional unit–*connective*—for the analysis of narrative structures in oral literature. A connective is a 'unit which connects parts of the narrative' (Jason, 1977, p. 104). A connective may be of two varieties:

a. An information connective: information is given

    1. by one character in the tale to another,

       (e.g., The old widow said to her three daughters, 'Girls, I have to go and attend a sacrificial feast at the village where our chief lives, and I shall be away for two or three days…' [Tale 19])

    2. by the narrator to the audience.

       (e.g., Once there lived an old man and old woman. They had no children, but had a cat living with them. [Tale 1])

b. A transfer connective in (1) state, (2) time, (3) space:

    1. transition in state (transformation from one state of being into another),

       (e.g., That night the snail changed into a little boy, and the ogress loved him as her own child. [Tale 25])

    2. transition in time (lapses of time without action),

       (e.g., For the next fortnight or two, the course of true love ran smoothly. [Tale 11])

    3. transition in space (transportations in space)

       (e.g., The little girl now jumped on to the mound, and it grew higher and higher. Finally the mound reached right up to the moon. [Tale 27])

Sometimes a connective is found to feature a character; however, it may exist without it. Unlike functional events, it can be fulfilled not only by a character's action but also by any event concerning one or several characters. Connectives should be regarded as another type of fundamental constituent, like functional events, which serves as a device through which tales are arranged into a well-organised storyline. With these additional units of moves and connectives, the study will illustrate various models of basic story structures in detail and explain the ways in which functional events are organised into a tale as a whole.

3.3. Analysis of the Linkage in a Storyline

The final phase of analysis will be on the linkage between the functional events of each model. Following Ochs and Capps' (2001) concept of linearity, the degree of temporal and/or causal linkage between events and moves constituting the storyline in each model will be analysed. According to Ochs and Capps (2001), the narrative dimension of linearity covers a span of possibilities for linking events into a unilinear time-line and cause-effect progression, and '[r]elatively linear narratives depict an overarching progression of events in which one event temporally precedes or causally leads to a subsequent event' (p. 41). Conversely, in relatively nonlinear narratives, the way in which one event relates to another temporally and causally is open-ended, in other words, 'open to vagaries of possibility, unpredictability, and indeterminacy' (Ochs & Capps, 2001, p. 83).

Folk tales have been regarded as a simple form of narrative (Genette, 1980; Toolan, 1988); in this connection, it is generally believed that the proclivities to construct an overarching storyline that ties events together in a seamless explanatory framework have been the focus of folklore (Ochs & Capps,

2001). With the analysis of the linkage between events, this study will examine how the storylines of Burmese folk tales contribute to such a proclivity of linking events, in order to create a plot structure with a relatively high degree of linearity.

As the present study will analyse the narrative structures of the folk tales in the form of text, the other dimensions will be assumed as defaults: tellership (one active teller), tellability (highly tellable account), embeddedness (relatively detached from surrounding talk and activity), and moral stance (certain, constant).

The degree of linearity between the functional events in the aforementioned sample tale, Tale 3, 'Why the Snail's Muscles Never Ache?', can be analysed as follows:

Events	*Linkage*
1. Lack or insufficiency in one of the protagonists. (Lack in Protagonist A)	Temporal/Causal Event 1 leads to Event 2.
2. Protagonist A meets Helper.	
3. Protagonist A attempts to harm Protagonist B with trickery.	Temporal/Causal Event 2 leads to Event 3.
4. Protagonist B submits to Protagonist A's trickery.	Temporal Event 3 anticipates Event 4.
5. Protagonist B complies with deceitful persuasion.	Causal Event 4 causes Event 5.
6. The victory of Protagonist A and the fall of Protagonist B.	Temporal/Causal Event 5 results in Event 6.

A high degree of linearity is uncovered in the storyline of the sample tale as one event anticipates, causes, or leads to another in a progressive, forward-moving timeline and cause-effect progression. In this structural pattern, events are linked within a highly linear plot structure with a beginning that builds to a middle and then is resolved in the ending. The narrative structures in other types of tales may not constitute the same functional events and the same type of linearity between events. They may not uniformly thread events into a unilinear time-line and cause-effect progression.

Although the combination sequence of functional events in a tale may not be identical to that of the other, as it is claimed in Propp's (1968) study, a highly linear plot structure will still prove a tale to be a linear, coherent narrative. According to Ochs and Capps (2001), '[l]inear, coherent narratives generally have a plot structure that depicts a sequence of temporally and causally ordered events organised around a point' (p. 4). The narrative dimension of linearity will measure not only the interconnectedness and sequentiality between events in each move, but also between two successive moves constituting the storyline of an entire tale.

Chapter 4

Analysis of Tales

Similar to Propp's study, the present study faces the problem of assimilation—'different functions fulfilled in exactly the same way' (Propp, 1968, p. 66). Hence, following Propp's suggestion, a functional event will be identified according to its consequences. Because the present study is not limited to only one type of tales, the results from the analysis will be listed against those suggested by Propp. In this way, the extent to which Propp's framework can be applied to the analysis of different types of tales can be explored. Detailed illustrations of each model will then be given with some sample tales, followed by the analyses of the linkage between events as well as between moves in each model.

4.1. Functional Events in Burmese Folk Tales

From the analyses of the 27 tales in the collection, various functional events are identified. Most of these functional events can be listed against Propp's 31 functional events. However, in individual cases, there are some actions of functional characters that do not conform to or are defined by any of the functional events mentioned in Propp's study. Thus, several new functional events have to be added to fit the study of different tale types. In table 2, such new functional events are highlighted with the *** symbol in the column for Propp's functional events as abbreviated by Lim, Tan, and Wee (2001).

TABLE 2. Functional events in Burmese folk tales.

Functional Events in Burmese Folk Tales	Propp's 31 Functional Events (Abbreviated)
A family member leaves the family.	1. Absence
An interdiction is addressed to Protagonist. A contract is made between two Protagonists.	2. Interdiction
Initial equilibrium or friendship between two Protagonists.	***
Interdiction is violated. Contract between two Protagonists is violated.	3. Violation
End of equilibrium. (Disequilibrium)	***
Interdiction is restored.	***
Equilibrium is reinstated.	***
Interdiction is kept. Protagonists keep the contract.	***
Equilibrium is maintained.	***
Protagonist makes an attempt at reconnaissance of the other Protagonist.	4. Reconnaissance
Protagonist gets information about the other Protagonist.	5. Delivery
Protagonist attempts to deceive the other Protagonist with trickery.	6. Trickery

(*continued on next page*)

TABLE 2. *(continued)*

Functional Events in Burmese Folk Tales	Propp's 31 Functional Events (Abbreviated)
The other Protagonist submits to the trickery.	7. Complicity
Protagonist causes harm or injury to the other Protagonist.	8. Villainy
A member of the family lacks something. Lack or insufficiency in Protagonist.	8a. Lack
Lack or insufficiency is made known.	9. Mediation
The other Protagonists attempt to liquidate/ eliminate lack or insufficiency of the Protagonist.	***
Protagonist agrees to counteract.	10. Beginning counteraction
Protagonist leaves home.	11. Departure
Protagonist is tested by the donor.	12. First functional event of the donor
Protagonist reacts to villainy. Protagonist reacts to trickery of the other Protagonist.	13. Protagonist's reaction
Protagonist receives a magical object. Protagonists receive an entity.	14. Receipt of a magical object
Protagonists are in dispute over the entity given by the donor.	***
Transfer to place where the lack is to be found. e.g., Protagonist meets the guide. Protagonist is led to the helper. Guide leads Protagonists to the donor.	15. Guidance
Protagonist is given false guidance. Guide fails to settle the dispute.	***
Two protagonists in competition.	16. Struggle
Protagonist is branded.	17. Branding
The victory of one Protagonist over the other.	18. Victory
Lack is liquidated. Object of the quest is obtained by the protagonist.	19. Liquidation

(continued on next page)

TABLE 2. *(continued)*

Functional Events in Burmese Folk Tales	Propp's 31 Functional Events (Abbreviated)
Lack remains. Protagonist in the original states.	***
Protagonist returns home.	20. Return
Protagonist is pursued.	21. Pursuit
Protagonist is saved by the helper.	22. Rescue
The victory of the protagonist is unrecognised.	23. Unrecognised arrival
Protagonist B presents claims of Protagonist A.	24. Unfounded claims
Difficult task is set. Donor sets protagonists tasks or tests.	25. Difficult task
Task is solved. Protagonist A performs tasks or tests successfully.	26. Solution
Protagonist B fails the test.	***
Protagonist A is recognised. Protagonist A is rewarded. Protagonist A is reinstated.	27. Recognition
Trickery is unmasked.	28. Exposure
Protagonist A appears in new state. Protagonist A unmasks disguise.	29. Transfiguration
Protagonist B who fails the test is punished.	30. Punishment
Marriage and rule of Protagonist A.	31. Wedding
Protagonist A returns service to the helper.	***
Decision is made for the entity by the Protagonist with victory. Decision is made for the dispute by the helper.	***

As can be seen from table 2, Propp's concept of functional events is, to a large extent, applicable to the analysis of different types of tales, although there are certain functional events that are not covered in his study. The list of functional events identified in the analyses of the tales selected for the present study covers a wider range, reflecting different tale types. Therefore, in the next phase of analysis, these functional events will be classified into various models, so that structural similarities and differences in different types of tales can be discussed.

4.2. Classification of Functional Events into Different Models

The functional events identified in the analyses of Burmese folk tales can be classified into the following different models, according to the similarities in their structural patterns and functional events, making up the main storyline.

1. Reward/punishment
2. Interdiction/violation
3. Problem/solution
4. Trickster tales
5. Fairy tales

4.2.1. Reward/Punishment Model

In this model, there are two protagonists—one behaves according to certain specific rules and is rewarded and the other breaks these rules and is punished. The four narrative roles in this model will be:

(1) Protagonist A
(2) Protagonist B
(3) Donor
(4) Guide

Protagonist A is the main character in the first move of the story, and Protagonist B in the second move. They are comparable and stand in contrast to each other. The donor role is distributed among several characters who set a test for the Protagonists. The elementary sequence of functional events for this model can be listed as follows:

Move 1

Information connective	Protagonist A is introduced.
Event 1	Guide leads Protagonist A to Donor.
Transfer connective	Transition in space and/or time.
Event 2	Protagonist A meets Donor.
Event 3	Donor sets Protagonist A tasks/tests.
Event 4	Protagonist A performs successfully.
Event 5	Protagonist A is rewarded.

Move 2

Information connective	Protagonist B is introduced. Protagonist B learns about Donor from Protagonist A.
Event 6	Guide leads Protagonist B to Donor.
Transfer connective	Transition in space and/or time.
Event 7	Protagonist B meets Donor.
Event 8	Donor sets Protagonist B tasks/tests.
Event 9	Protagonist B fails.
Event 10	Protagonist B is punished. (Protagonist B is not rewarded.)

Analysis of a Sample Tale

Tale 7: 'The Golden Crow'

The distribution of characters in narrative roles:

Protagonist A: Good-Natured Girl
Protagonist B: Bad-Tempered Girl
Donor: Golden Crow
Guide: Tray of Paddy

'The Golden Crow'[4]	Events
Long ago, there lived an old widow who was very poor. She had a daughter who was pretty and good-natured.	Move 1 Information connective—Protagonist A is introduced.
One day, the mother asked the daughter to scare away the birds from the tray of paddy which was being dried in the sun. So the daughter sat down near the tray and scared away the birds. When the paddy was nearly dried, however, a strange bird came flying towards the tray. It was a crow with gold feathers. The Golden Crow laughed at the little girl's efforts to scare him away and quickly ate up every bit of the rice, chaff and all.	Event 1. Guide leads Protagonist A to Donor.
The girl started to cry, saying, 'Oh, my mother is so poor! My mother is so poor! The rice is so valuable to her'.	
The Golden Crow gave her a kindly look and said, 'Little girl, I will pay for it. Come to the big tamarind tree outside the village at sunset, and I will give you something'. Then the crow flew away.	
At sunset, the little girl went to the big tamarind tree and looked up at the branches. To her surprise, she saw a little house of gold at the top.	Transfer connective

(*continued on next page*)

(*continued*)

'The Golden Crow'[4]	Events
The crow looked out of a window of the little golden house, and said, 'Oh, there you are! Do come up. But, of course, I must drop the ladder first. Do you want the golden ladder, the silver ladder, or the brass ladder?'	Event 2. Protagonist A meets Donor. Event 3. Donor sets Protagonist A the first task/test.
'I am only a poor little girl', replied the girl, 'and I can only ask for the brass ladder'. To her surprise, the crow put down the golden ladder, and the little girl climbed up on it to the little gold house.	Event 4. Protagonist A performs successfully.
'You must have dinner with me', invited the crow. 'But let me see, do you want the gold dish, the silver dish, or the brass dish to eat your food from?'	Event 3. Donor sets Protagonist A the second task/test.
'I am only a poor little girl', she replied, 'and I can only ask for the brass dish'. To her surprise, the crow brought out the gold dish, and the food in it was delicious.	Event 4. Protagonist A performs successfully.
'You are a good little girl', said the crow, when the little girl had finished eating, 'and I would like you to stay here with me forever. But your mother needs you more, so I must send you back before it gets too dark'.	
Then he went into the bedroom and brought out a big box, a medium-sized box, and a small box. 'Choose one of these boxes', said the crow, 'and give it to your mother'.	Event 3. Donor sets Protagonist A the third task/test.
'The paddy you ate was not much', replied the girl, 'and the little box would be more than enough'. She then accepted the little box and, after thanking the Golden Crow, climbed down the golden ladder and went home.	Event 4. Protagonist A performs successfully.
When she reached there, she gave the little box to her mother. Together they opened it, and they were surprised and delighted to find in the box a hundred priceless rubies. The mother and daughter became very rich and lived in luxury.	Event 5. Protagonist A is rewarded.

(*continued on next page*)

(*continued*)

'The Golden Crow'[4]	**Events**
There was another old widow in the village, but she was not poor. She also had a daughter who, however, was greedy and bad-tempered. This widow and her daughter heard about the gift of the Golden Crow, and became very jealous of the other widow and her daughter.	<u>Move 2</u> Information connective—Protagonist B is introduced. Protagonist B learns about Donor.
They decided to try to get a similar gift for themselves. So they put out a tray of paddy in the sun, and the greedy girl kept watch. But as she was lazy, she did not try to scare away the birds that came to eat up the paddy. When the Golden Crow at last turned up, there were very few grains left.	Event 6. Guide leads Protagonist B to Donor.
However, the Golden Crow ate what remained, and the greedy girl shouted rudely, 'Hey, crow, give me and my mother some wealth for the paddy you have eaten'.	
The crow looked at her with a frown, but he replied politely enough, 'Little girl, I will pay for the rice. Come to the big tamarind tree outside the village at sunset, and I will give you something'. Then the crow flew away.	
At sunset, the greedy girl went to the big tamarind tree and, without waiting for the crow to come out, she shouted, 'Hey, crow, keep your promise'.	Transfer connective Event 7. Protagonist B meets Donor.
The crow put his head out of the window and asked, 'On which ladder do you want to climb up here? The golden ladder, the silver ladder, or the brass ladder?'	Event 8. Donor sets Protagonist B the first task/test.
'The golden ladder, of course', replied the greedy girl. But, to her disappointment, the crow lowered the brass ladder.	Event 9. Protagonist B fails.
When the girl entered the little gold house, the crow said, 'You must dine with me. Do you want to eat your food from the gold dish, the silver dish, or the brass dish?'	Event 8. Donor sets Protagonist B the second task/test.

(*continued on next page*)

(*continued*)

'The Golden Crow'[4]	Events
'The gold dish, of course', replied the greedy girl. But to her disappointment, it was the brass dish she was served. The food was delicious but it was no more than a tiny morsel, and the greedy girl was annoyed.	Event 9. Protagonist B fails.
Then the crow went into the bedroom and brought out a big box, a medium-sized box, and a small box, and said, 'Choose one of these boxes and give it to your mother'.	Event 8. Donor sets Protagonist B the third task/test.
The greedy girl, of course, chose the big box, and without remembering to thank the crow, she struggled down the ladder with her burden.	Event 9. Protagonist B fails.
When she reached home, she and her mother joyfully pulled open the big box. But to their surprise and terror, a big snake lay coiled inside. The snake hissed at them angrily and then glided out of the box and out of their house.	Event 10. Protagonist B is punished. (Protagonist B is not rewarded.)

As illustrated in the sample analysis, the elementary sequence of functional events in the reward/punishment model consists of 'two symmetrically opposed moves, which are formally identical' (Drory, 1977, p. 32). The structure of this model can be summarised as

Tasks → Success → Reward (or)
Tasks → Failure → Punishment

Out of the 27 tales in the collection, the following four tales are found to have a storyline with the reward/punishment model.

Tale 7: 'The Golden Crow'
Tale 8: 'The Drunkard and the Opium Eater'

Tale 15: 'The Drunkard and the Threatening Ghost'
Tale 23: 'The Magic Cock'

The functional events identified in Tale 23, 'The Magic Cock', are similar to those identified in Tale 7, 'The Golden Crow'. In Tale 23, although there are four brothers who appear in the tale as characters, the narrative roles are distributed as follows:

Protagonist A: The Fourth Brother
Protagonist B: Three Brothers (taking one narrative role together)
Donor: Magic Cock
Guide: White Buffalo

Move 1

Information connective	Protagonists are introduced.
Event 1	Guide leads Protagonist A to Donor. The fourth brother rode on the white buffalo and started on a journey during which he would meet a wizard who would exchange the magic cock for his white buffalo.
Transfer connective	Transition in space and/or time.
Event 2	Protagonist A meets Donor. The fourth brother received the magic cock from the wizard in return for his white buffalo.
Event 3	Donor sets Protagonist A tasks/tests. The magic cock blew strong wind, mist, cloud, and a hail storm.

Event 4	Protagonist A performs successfully. The fourth brother tried to protect the magic cock by covering it with his body.
Event 5	Protagonist A is rewarded. The fourth brother was crowned as the king in a golden city.

Move 2

Transfer connective	Transition in time (after some months)
Information connective	Protagonist B (the three brothers) learned about the magic cock from Protagonist A (the fourth brother).
Event 7	Protagonist B meets Donor. The three brothers received the magic cock from the fourth brother.
Event 8	Donor sets Protagonist B tasks/tests. The magic cock blew a great hail storm.
Event 9	Protagonist B fails. The three brothers fled to a nearby cave for shelter, leaving the magic cock to be killed by the hail stones.
Event 10	Protagonist B is punished. (Protagonist B is not rewarded.) The three brothers had to continue living as 'strolling players'.

Unlike Tales 7 and 23, Tale 15, 'The Drunkard and the Threatening Ghost', is made up of only one move—Move 1—in which the protagonist (the drunkard) successfully drives away the threatening ghosts, which was the task set by the donor (the merchant who owned a haunted house). The tale ends when the drunkard is rewarded with the ownership of the house.

Conversely, Tale 8, 'The Drunkard and the Opium Eater', has an additional move—Move 3. In Move 1, Protagonist A (the drunkard) successfully performed the test of not letting his presence be discovered by the ghosts, and was rewarded with pots of gold. In Move 2, Protagonist B (the opium eater) failed the same test and the ghosts pulled his nose as a punishment until it became three yards long. In the additional move, Move 3, Protagonist A (the drunkard) attempts to help Protagonist B (the opium eater) by going through the test of not letting his presence be discovered by the ghosts for the second time. Thus, in addition to the functional events identified previously in Move 1 and Move 2, the following additional functional events are identified in Move 3 in Tale 8.

Move 3

Information connective	Protagonist A learns about the failure of Protagonist B.
	The drunkard went to look for his friend at the rest house the next morning and found him feeling shocked and scared.
Event 11	Protagonist A attempts to help Protagonist B.
	The drunkard consoled his friend and promised him that he would go and see the ghosts again and find out the cure for the long nose.
Event 12	Protagonist A meets Donor again.
	That night, the drunkard went to the cemetery rest house again and waited until two or three ghosts came in.

Event 13 Donor sets Protagonist A tasks.

One ghost suggested that the company be carefully counted because he could smell human flesh.

Event 14 Protagonist A performs successfully.

The drunkard stood up and shouted, 'One, two, three, four!...All correct, all correct'. The ghosts believed him, and started to talk.

Event 15 Protagonist A is rewarded.

The ghosts gave the drunkard the remedy to make a long nose become the right length again.

Event 16 Protagonist B is helped by Protagonist A.

The drunkard gave the remedy to his friend, the opium eater. The opium eater's nose became the right size again.

Table 3 summarises the distribution of the 16 functional events as they have been identified in these four tales with the reward/punishment model.

TABLE 3. Functional events (E) in the tales with reward/punishment model.

Tale no.	E 1	E 2	E 3	E 4	E 5	E 6	E 7	E 8	E 9	E 10	E 11	E 12	E 13	E 14	E 15	E 16
7	#	#	#	#	#	#	#	#	#	#						
8		#	#	#	#		#	#	#	#	#	#	#	#	#	#
15	#	#	#	#	#											
23	#	#	#	#	#		#	#	#	#						

4.2.2. Interdiction/Violation Model

Of the several structural patterns in Burmese folk tales, one of them can be classified according to the interdiction/violation model. In this model, the violation of an interdiction or a contract between the two protagonists will lead to a movement from equilibrium to disequilibrium or from friendship to a lack of friendship. Conversely, the preservation of an interdiction or a contract between the two protagonists will lead to the continuation of equilibrium or friendship. Thus, the structure of those tales with the interdiction/violation model can be summarised as

'Interdiction → Preservation → Equilibrium maintained' (or)
'Interdiction → Violation → Disequilibrium'

The functional events of this model can be outlined as follows:

Narrative roles:

1. Protagonist A
2. Protagonist B

Move 1

Information connective	Protagonists are introduced.
Event 1	Equilibrium or friendship between the Protagonists.
Event 2	An interdiction is made between Protagonist A and Protagonist B.
Transfer connective	Transition in time and/or space.
Event 3	Protagonist B is tested.
Event 4a	Interdiction is kept.

Event 4b	Interdiction is violated.
Transfer connective	Transition in time and/or space.
Event 5a	Equilibrium or friendship is maintained.
Event 5b	Discovery of violation, the end of equilibrium or friendship.

Analysis of a Sample Tale

The following is the analysis of a sample tale with the interdiction/violation model in which the interdiction is violated.

Tale 13: 'The Great King Eats Chaff'

Distribution of characters in narrative roles:

Protagonist A: The King
Protagonist B: The Attendant

'The Great King Eats Chaff'[5]	Events
The great king, with only one attendant, went incognito for a stroll in his city. He stopped to watch an old woman pounding paddy. The chaff which the old woman threw away after her pounding smelt very sweet, and the king was seized with an overmastering desire to eat it. He walked on for a few yards, and then ordered his attendant to go back and bring some of the chaff as he wanted to eat it. The attendant was shocked and protested that it was a disgraceful thing for a great king to eat chaff, which was food fit only for cows and pigs. But the king refused to see reason. So the chaff had to be fetched, and the king ate it with relish. Then the great king said to the attendant, 'If you tell about this to anyone, off goes your head'.	Move 1 Information connective—Protagonists are introduced. Event 2. An interdiction is made.

(*continued on next page*)

(*continued*)

'The Great King Eats Chaff'[5]	**Events**
When the attendant reached home, he was seized with an itch to tell. He tried to eat, he tried to sleep, and he tried to sing, but to no purpose, the itch to tell remained. 'If only I could whisper it out', he thought. Two or three days passed, and the attendant became ill and haggard, but the itch to tell still tortured him. At last, unable to bear it any longer, he rushed out of his house in search of a secluded spot where he could whisper out what he wanted to say, without anybody hearing him. He rowed himself in a boat mid-river, but he thought the fisherman would hear him. He went to the cemetery, but he thought the gravedigger would hear him.	Transfer connective—Transition in space. Event 3. Protagonist B is tested.
In the end, he went to the forest and, putting his head in the hollow of a big tree, whispered fervently, 'The great king eats chaff. The great king eats chaff. The great king eats chaff'. He felt better and returned home.	Event 4b. Interdiction is violated.
Many months later, the big palace drum, which announced the hours to the people, becoming too old to remain serviceable for long, a new drum had to be ordered. The drummakers went to the forest and cut down a big tree to use its wood for the new drum. It happened that the tree they cut down was the very tree in the hollow of which the attendant had whispered out his secret. At last, the new drum was ready. It was a beautiful thing. The drummakers looked at it, the people looked at it, the palace officials looked at it, and the great king looked at it; and all were satisfied. With great ceremony, and before a huge crowd of people, the new drum was installed; but when the drum was beaten, it did not say 'boom, boom' as is usual with all drums, but said instead, 'The great king eats chaff. The great king eats chaff'.	Transfer connective—Transition in time and space. Event 5b. Discovery of violation and end of equilibrium.

Tale 11, 'Not Angry, but Buffalo Tails Have Become Short', and Tale 18, 'Why Female Elephants Hate Pregnant Women', are found to have the similar narrative structures of the interdiction/violation model. In Tale 18, the Female Elephant and the Pregnant Woman are distributed to the narrative roles of Protagonist A and Protagonist B, respectively. The following functional events are identified in Tale 18:

Information connective	Protagonists are introduced.
Event 1	Equilibrium or friendship between the Protagonists.
	The female elephant came to the woman for advice and discussed the matter of marriage with the woman.
Event 2	An interdiction is made between Protagonist A and Protagonist B.
	The woman told the female elephant that she had to carry the child in her womb for twenty months. The female elephant believed what the woman said and carried her child in her womb for twenty months before giving birth to it.
Event 3	Protagonist B is tested.
	The woman was pregnant.
Event 4b	Interdiction is violated.
	The woman carried the child in her womb only for ten months.
Event 5b	Discovery of violation, the end of equilibrium or friendship.

> The female elephant was furious when she made this discovery. All descendants of the female elephant harbour resentment against pregnant women.

In Tale 11, 'Not Angry, but Buffalo Tails Have Become Short', unlike Tales 13 and 18, the interdiction made between the two protagonists is kept, and the equilibrium or friendship is maintained. Therefore, the functional events (4a) and (5a), instead of (4b) and (5b), are identified in Tale 11. The functional events and a summary of the tale are listed next.

Tale 11: 'Not Angry, but Buffalo Tails Have Become Short'

Distribution of characters in narrative roles:

Protagonist A: The Farmer
Protagonist B: The Son-In-Law

Move 1

Information connective	Protagonists (the farmer and the son-in-law) are introduced.
Event 2	An interdiction is made between Protagonist A and Protagonist B. The farmer told his wife that he would give his consent to the marriage of their daughter and the young man if their future son-in-law agreed to never lose his temper under any circumstances. The young man agreed and was married to the farmer's daughter.
Transfer connective	Transition in time. A fortnight or two passed.

Event 3 Protagonist B is tested.

One day, when the daughter was preparing to leave for the field with her husband's lunch as usual, the farmer forbade her to go. The farmer made his daughter late for more than two hours.

Event 4a Interdiction is kept.

The son-in-law, while waiting for his wife with his meal, cut off the tips of the tails of the grazing buffaloes, roasted and ate them to overcome his hunger. When his wife finally arrived over two hours later, the young man was still as even-tempered as before. He told his wife that he was not angry with her. Only the tails of the buffaloes had become shorter.

Event 5a Equilibrium or friendship is maintained.

The young man continued to be the farmer's son-in-law. The farmer was kind to him as the young man remained as even-tempered as before.

Tale 21, 'The Origin of Fire', has the similar narrative structures of the interdiction/violation model. An interdiction was made between Protagonist A (the Villager) and Protagonist B (Wa Magum, the great god). The following are the functional events identified in Tale 21.

Information connective Protagonists are introduced.

Event 2 An interdiction is made between Protagonist A and Protagonist B.

	Wa Magum, the great god, permitted the villager to take away the god of fire, but he warned him to be cautious and to call a man and a woman in order to have them rub two pieces of bamboo together should the fire ever go out.
Transfer connective	Transition in time and/or place. The long months of winter passed.
Event 3	Protagonist B is tested. The villager (his friend and fellow villagers) no longer needed the fire to warm themselves.
Event 4b	Interdiction is violated. The fire was forgotten, and it was left to burn the whole village and then to burn itself out.
Event 5b	Discovery of violation, the end of equilibrium or friendship. The villagers cursed the fire and drove out the villager and his friend who first brought the fire to the village.

However, unlike Tales 11 and 13, Tale 21 has an additional move, which includes the following additional functional events.

Move 2

Transfer connective	Transition in time and/or space Winter months came around again.
Event 6	Protagonist is pursued. The villager and his friend were asked to look for the great god and the god of fire.

TABLE 4. Functional events (E) in the tales with interdiction/violation model.

Tale no.	E 1	E 2	E 3	E 4a	E 4b	E 5a	E 5b	E 6	E 7	E 8
11		#	#	#		#				
13		#	#		#		#			
18	#	#	#		#		#			
21		#	#		#		#	#	#	#

Event 7 Interdiction is restored.

They recalled the words of the great god to call a man and a woman and to have them rub two pieces of bamboo together should the fire go out.

Event 8 Equilibrium is reinstated.

A man and a woman were called. Sparks from the two pieces of bamboo rubbed by them became fire brands. All the villagers had the company of the god of fire again.

Table 4 summarises the distribution of all these eight functional events, as identified in the four tales with the interdiction/violation model.

4.2.3. Problem/Solution Model

The collection of Burmese folk tales selected for the present study includes some tales that are categorised as 'Law tale' by the collector. A particular pattern of functional events is found in the narrative structures of these tales. This pattern can be classified as the problem/solution model. The narrative roles for this model are:

1. Protagonist A
2. Protagonist B
3. Object of dispute
4. Guide
5. Helper

The functional events making up the storyline with this model can be outlined as follows:

Information connective	Protagonists are introduced.
Event 1	Protagonist A meets Protagonist B.
Event 2	Protagonist A and Protagonist B are in dispute over an object.
Event 3	Protagonist A and Protagonist B meets Guide.
Event 4	Guide fails to settle the dispute.
Transfer connective	Transition in time and/or space.
Event 5	Protagonists meet Helper.
Event 6	Helper makes decision.

Analysis of a Sample Tale

Tale 17: 'The Greedy Stall Keeper and the Poor Traveller'

Distribution of characters to narrative roles:

Protagonist A: The Greedy Stall-Keeper
Protagonist B: The Poor Traveller
Object for dispute: Fried Fish Smell
Guide: The Crowd
Helper: The Princess Learned-in-the-Law

'The Greedy Stall-Keeper and the Poor Traveller'[6]	Events
A poor traveller stopped under a tree to eat his simple meal, which he had brought with him in a bundle. The meal consisted only of some cooked rice and boiled vegetables. It was the cool season, during which people travelled from one village to another, and there were many wayside stalls selling fried fish and fried cakes.	Information connective—Protagonists are introduced.
A few yards away to the north from where the poor traveller was eating his meal, there stood a food-stall at which the owner was frying some fish. She carefully watched the traveller eating his meal, and when the latter had finished, she demanded, 'Give me a silver quarter, for the	Event 1. Protagonist A meets Protagonist B.
fried fish'. 'But, Mistress', protested the poor traveller, 'I have not even come near your stall, let alone take some fish from you'. 'You miser, you cheat', shouted the woman, 'everybody can see that you have been enjoying your meal with the smell of my fried fish. Without the smell, your meal consisting merely of rice and salt could not have been so tasty'.	Event 2. Protagonist A and Protagonist B are in dispute over an object.
A crowd soon collected, and although the sympathy was with the poor traveller, all had to admit that as the wind was blowing from the north, it must have carried the smell from the frying-pan to the traveller.	Event 3. Protagonist A and Protagonist B meet Guide. Event 4. Guide fails to settle the dispute.
Finally, the woman and the traveller went before the Princess Learned-in-the-Law, and she passed the following judgment.	Event 5. Protagonists meet Helper.
'The woman insists that the traveller ate his meal with the smell of her fried fish. The traveller cannot deny that the wind did carry the smell of frying fish to his nostrils as he sat eating. Therefore, he must pay the price. But what was the price of fried fish? The woman says it is fixed at a silver quarter for each plate of fried fish. Let the woman and the traveller go out of the court into the sunlight; let the traveller	Event 6. Helper makes decision.

(*continued on next page*)

(*continued*)

'The Greedy Stall-Keeper and the Poor Traveller'[6]	**Events**
hold out a silver quarter, and let the woman take the shadow cast by that silver quarter. For if the price of a plate of fried fish is a silver quarter, the price of the *smell* of a plate of fried fish must be the shadow of a silver quarter'.	

Tale 16, 'The Poor Scholar and the Alchemist', is found to have the same structural pattern of the problem/solution model. The narrative roles and functional events in Tale 16 are as follows:

Protagonist A: The Alchemist Protagonist B: The Poor Scholar
Object of dispute: The Beautiful Maiden
Guide: The Goddess of the Pond
Helper: The Princess Learned-in-the-Law

Information connective	Protagonists are introduced.
Event 1	Protagonist A meets Protagonist B. The alchemist met the poor scholar who had just graduated and was on his journey home with the professor's daughter, the beautiful maiden, who was rewarded to him for his excellent work.
Event 2	Protagonist A and Protagonist B are in dispute over an object. The alchemist fell in love with the young maiden. The alchemist and the scholar attacked

each other with swords. They simultaneously cut off each other's head.

Event 3 — Protagonist A and Protagonist B meets Guide.

The goddess of the pond appeared and placed each head on a lifeless trunk. Both the alchemist and the scholar became alive.

Event 4 — Guide fails to settle the dispute.

The goddess had placed each head on the wrong trunk. Both men (with their heads on the wrong trunks) claimed the beautiful maiden as their wife.

Event 5 — Protagonists meet Helper.

The alchemist, the scholar, and the young maiden were taken to the Princess Learned-in-the-Law.

Event 6 — Helper makes decision.

The Princess Learned-in-the-Law decided that the man with the scholar's head was the legal husband of the beautiful maiden because 'a man's personality was in the head'.

TABLE 5. Functional events (E) in the tales with problem/solution model.

Tale no.	E. 1	E. 2	E. 3	E. 4	E. 5	E. 6
16	#	#	#	#	#	#
17	#	#	#	#	#	#

Table 5 shows the distribution of these functional events identified in Tales 16 and 17.

4.2.4. Trickster Tales

One of the prominent structural patterns in Burmese folk tales is the model for the trickster tale. In this model, the main characters will play the narrative roles of two protagonists, one trying to deceive the other with trickery. The other protagonist, on whom the trick is played, either submits or reacts to it. The trickery is resolved with the victory of one of the protagonists, either the one who deceives or who is deceived.

The narrative roles for this model are:

1. Protagonist A
2. Protagonist B
3. Helper

The elementary sequence of functional events in a move with this model can be listed as follows:

Information connective	Protagonists are introduced.
Event 1	Lack or insufficiency in one of the protagonists.
Event 2	One protagonist meets the helper.
Event 3	One protagonist attempts to harm the other with trickery.
Event 4a	The other protagonist submits to trickery.
Event 4b	The other protagonist reacts (with more trickery).

Event 5a	The other protagonist complies with the deceitful persuasions.
Event 5b	Two protagonists in competition.
Event 6a	The victory of the protagonist who plays the trick.
Event 6b	The victory of the protagonist who reacts.
Event 7	Resolution (various forms of resolution are found). – Discovery of the trickery. – The protagonist with the victory makes decision for an entity. – The protagonist with the victory is recognised by the defeated protagonist.

Analysis of a Sample Tale

Tale 10: 'Jealous of Others, Suffer Own Loss'

Distribution of characters to narrative roles:

Protagonist A: The Washerman
Protagonist B: The Potter

Information connective	Protagonists (the washerman and the potter) are introduced.
Event 1	Lack or insufficiency in one of the Protagonists. The potter became poorer while the washerman gradually grew prosperous.
Event 3	One protagonist attempts to harm the other with trickery.

	The potter became jealous and set a plan to ruin the washerman by exclaiming to the king that the king's royal black elephant should be washed clean and turned into a white one by the washerman.
Event 4b	The other protagonist reacts (with another trickery).
	The washerman was an intelligent man and immediately realized that it was the jealous potter who had approached the king. The washerman replied to the king that it was a great honour and a great pleasure to wash the king's royal black elephant. But the washerman pointed out that he would need a pot large enough to hold the elephant so that it could be steamed after being washed.
Event 5b	Two protagonists in competition.
	The jealous potter had to spend many days making a large pot. When it was ready, the washerman after washing the elephant, put the animal into the pot. The moment the elephant stepped into the pot, it broke into pieces under the animal's weight.
Event 6b	The victory of the protagonist who reacts.
	The king ordered the potter to make another pot, and yet another pot. This went on and on until the potter was completely ruined and died of a heart attack.

Similarly, Tale 3, 'Why the Snail's Muscles Never Ache?' (the sample analysis in 3.1.1), is an example of a trickster tale in which the protagonist who reacts succeeds in the end. The storyline of a trickster tale can be summarised as:

Trickery → Submission → Complicity → Victory (of the Protagonist who plays the trick)

(or)

Trickery → Counteraction → Competition → Victory (of the Protagonist who reacts)

Out of the 27 tales in the collection, the following are found to have a structural pattern similar to the model for a trickster tale.

Tale 1: 'The Cat Who Pretended to Be a University Professor'
Tale 2: 'The Lapwing and the Lay Brother'
Tale 3: 'Why the Snail's Muscles Never Ache?'
Tale 5: 'Mister Luck and Mister Industry'
Tale 10: 'Jealous of Others, Suffer Own Loss'
Tale 12: 'How the Opium Eater Went to Heaven?' [*sic*]
Tale 20: 'When the Gods Played Hide and Seek'

However, it is noted that there are some slight differences among the structural patterns of these tales with the trickster tale model. For example, Tale 1, 'The Cat Who Pretended to Be a University Professor', consists of six main characters. One of them, the cat, plays the role of Protagonist A who tries to deceive Protagonists B, C, D, E, and F (the old man, water duck, water fowl, crow, and pheasant) one at a time. Therefore, the structural pattern of this tale consists of a series of moves, with the recurrence of the following functional events in sequence.

Move 1

Event 3	Protagonist A attempts to harm Protagonist B with trickery. The cat ate up all the meat that the old woman had cooked for the morning and evening meals, but he pretended to be innocent and made the old woman protest when the old man suspected him to be the thief.
Event 4b	Protagonist B reacts (with trickery). The old man bought pots with very narrow necks and asked his wife to put the meat in them.
Event 5b	Two protagonists in competition. The old man caught the cat with his head inside the pot as the cat could not get his head out of the narrow neck after eating the meat in it. The cat struggled to free himself.
Event 6b	The victory of the protagonist who reacts. The old man aimed a blow at the cat with a stick, but it missed the mark and hit the pot instead. The cat had to flee to a forest with the rim of the pot stuck around his neck.

Move 2

Event 3	Protagonist A attempts to harm Protagonist C with trickery. The cat, now with the rim of the pot around the neck that made him look like a professor with a royal insignia of learning around the neck, pretended to be a university professor

	and invited the water duck to his chamber for special lessons on medicine.
Event 4a	Protagonist C submits to trickery.
	The water duck was greatly impressed.
Event 5a	Protagonist C complies with the deceitful persuasions.
	The water duck presented himself at the cat's chamber.
Event 6a	The victory of the protagonist who plays the trick.
	The water duck was eaten up by the cat.

Move 3

Event 3	Protagonist A attempts to harm Protagonist D with trickery.
	The cat, now with the rim of the pot around the neck that made him look like a professor with a royal insignia of learning around the neck, pretended to be a university professor and invited the water fowl to his chamber for special lessons on law.
Event 4a	Protagonist D submits to trickery.
	The water fowl was greatly impressed.
Event 5a	Protagonist D complies with the deceitful persuasions.
	The water fowl presented himself at the cat's chamber.
Event 6a	The victory of the Protagonist who plays the trick.
	The water fowl was eaten up by the cat.

Move 4

Event 3 Protagonist A attempts to harm Protagonist E with trickery.

The cat, now with the rim of the pot around the neck that made him look like a professor with a royal insignia of learning around the neck, pretended to be a university professor and invited the crow to his chamber for special lessons on literary studies.

Event 4b Protagonist E reacts (with trickery).

The crow went to the cat's chamber with his close friend, the pheasant, who waited outside the door while the crow presented himself to the cat.

Event 5b Two Protagonists in competition.

The cat attempted to eat the crow, but the pheasant rushed inside and together with the crow attacked the cat.

Event 6b The victory of the Protagonist who reacts.

The cat jumped down, ran into the stream, and drowned.

TABLE 6. Functional events (E) in Tale 1 (trickster tale, with four moves).

Move	E. 1	E. 2	E. 3	E. 4a	E. 4b	E. 5a	E. 5b	E. 6a	E. 6b	E. 7
1			#		#		#		#	
2			#	#		#		#		
3			#	#		#		#		
4			#		#		#		#	

Table 6 summarises the distribution of these functional events in the four moves identified in Tale 1.

In Tale 2, 'The Lapwing and the Lay Brother', there are only two Protagonists:

Protagonist A: The Lapwing
Protagonist B: The Lay Brother

The functional events identified in Tale 2 are listed as follows:

Event 1	Lack or insufficiency in one of the protagonists. The lay brother of a monastery was eccentric and easily annoyed.
Event 3	Protagonist A attempts to harm Protagonist B with trickery. The lapwing taunted the lay brother by calling him a fool, in order to make him break his vow that he would not harm any living creature.
Event 4a	Protagonist B submits to trickery. The lay brother was angry, and he chased and caught the bird.
Event 5a	Protagonist B complies with the deceitful persuasions. Following the bird's taunts, the lay brother plucked off his feathers, killed the bird, and cooked and ate it.
Event 6a	The victory of the protagonist who plays the trick. The bird flew out from the lay brother's mouth and sang that he had fooled the lay brother.

Similarly, in Tale 5, 'Mister Luck and Mister Industry', the two protagonists are (A) Mister Luck and (B) Mister Industry. The functional events identified in this tale similarly follow the sequence of 'Trickery → Submission → Complicity → Victory'. However, Protagonist A's trickery of turning someone into a monkey and then back into a human being was imposed on a victim (the princess) instead of Protagonist B. Protagonist A's victory was in the form of winning the princess's hand and being crowned as the king. The tale ends with an additional functional event—Event 7 (Resolution)—in which Protagonist B (Mister Industry) acknowledged the victory of Protagonist A (Mister Luck).

Conversely, Tale 12, 'How the Opium Eater Went to Heaven?', includes three protagonists.

Protagonist A: The Opium Eater
Protagonist B: The Lord Judge
Protagonist C: The Old Man

The functional events in Tale 12 are identified as follows:

Move 1

Information connective	Protagonists are introduced.
Event 1	Lack or insufficiency in Protagonist A. The opium eater had no record for a great deed of merit to convince the lord judge that he should not be sent to hell.
Event 3	Protagonist A attempts to deceive Protagonist B with trickery. The opium eater told the lord judge that he did *bushein.* The opium eater was using the

	spoonerism for *beinshu*, which means 'smoke opium' in Burmese.
Event 4a	Protagonist B submits to trickery.
	The lord judge thought *bushein* was a term in Pali, the classical language of Buddhism in which he was not fluent.
Event 5a	Protagonist B complies with the deceitful persuasions.
	The lord judge thought that it must be an important deed of merit to have a Pali reference, and told the guard to put the opium eater on the middle tier of the chariot to be sent to heaven while he would go and ask the king of gods for advice.
Event 6a	The victory of the Protagonist who plays the trick.
	The guard put the opium eater on the middle tier of the chariot.

Move 2

Transfer connective	Transition in place and/or time.
Event 3	Protagonist A attempts to harm Protagonist C with trickery.
	The opium eater told the old man sitting on the lower tier of the chariot that the old man—for being a very considerate person with charming manners—deserved to be on the middle tier.
Event 4a	Protagonist C submits to trickery.

	The old man was convinced that the lord judge must have misjudged the nature of his deeds of merit.
Event 5a	Protagonist C complies with the deceitful persuasions.
	The old man agreed to change seats with the opium eater.
Event 6a	The victory of Protagonist A.
	The opium eater managed to change his seat to the lower tier before the lord judge returned from the king of gods.
Event 7	Resolution (discovery of the trickery).
	The lord judge found out from the king of gods about the spoonerism.
Event 4b	Protagonist B reacts.
	The lord judge angrily pulled down the person sitting on the middle tier of the chariot and threw him into hell.
Event 6a	The victory of Protagonist A, who plays the trick.
	The opium eater, who had moved to the lower tier of the chariot, was carried to heaven.

The last tale with a trickster tale model is Tale 20, 'When the Gods Played Hide and Seek'. The characters are distributed to the two narrative roles of Protagonists A and B, and the following functional events are identified.

Protagonist A: The Rain God
Protagonist B: The Sky God

Move 1

Information connective	Protagonists are introduced.
Event 3	Protagonist A attempts to deceive Protagonist B.
	The rain god hid himself inside the bowels of the earth.
Event 4b	The other protagonist reacts.
	The sky god spied the rain god well and saw him curling up in the bowels of the earth.
Event 6b	The victory of the protagonist who reacts.
	The sky god shouted to the rain god to come out from his hiding place.

Move 2

Event 3	Protagonist B attempts to deceive Protagonist A.
	The sky god hid himself inside the rain god's ear.
Event 4a	The other Protagonist submits to trickery.
	The rain god looked for the sky god everywhere else.
Event 5a	The other Protagonist complies with the deceitful persuasions.
	The rain god could not find the sky god and gave up on the game.
Event 6a	The victory of the Protagonist who plays the trick.

	The sky god came out from the rain god's ear and claimed that he was really a very powerful god.
Event 7	Resolution (The Protagonist with the victory makes decision for an entity).
	The sky god decided that he would rule over the more cultured and cunning people, and he asked the rain god to rule the less cultured, more simple, and honest people.

4.2.5. Fairy Tales

The storylines of certain tales in the collection are found to comprise functional events that match most of the 31 functional events found in the Russian fairy tales studied by Propp. The structures of these tales also share some properties of a fairy tale, such as miraculous transformations (Zipes, 2000). Their storylines consist of several moves that are joined by transfer connectives. Tales with such storylines will be classified as Burmese fairy tales. The elementary storyline for the tales with the fairy tale model can be analysed using Propp's 31 functional events, which have been listed in table 2 (pp. 34–36).

Analysis of a Sample Tale

Tale 6: 'How Master Thumb Defeated the Sun?' [*sic*]

Distribution of characters to narrative roles:

Villain 1: The Sun   Protagonist (hero): Master Thumb
Villain 2: Ogre   Magical objects: The Rice Cake
Helper: Boat, Bamboo Thorn, Moss, Rotten Egg, Rain

'How Master Thumb Defeated the Sun?'[7]	**Events**
Once a poor woman, who was expecting, was trying to dry some paddy. But the moment she put out her basket of paddy the sun disappeared, and the moment she took in her basket thinking it was going to rain, the sun shone bright and clear again. This was repeated so many times that the woman lost her temper and abused the sun. The sun in return laid upon her a curse, with the result that when her son was born he was no bigger than a man's thumb. The child was given the name of Master Thumb.	Move 1 Information connective—Protagonist is introduced.
Master Thumb felt very unhappy because other children made fun of his small stature and when he reached the age of sixteen years, he demanded of his mother the true reason for his being no bigger than a thumb. When he learned that the sun's curse was the cause, he said, 'Mother, make me a rice cake tomorrow, for I am going in search of the sun to fight him'.	Event 8a. Lack Event 9. Mediation
Early next morning, Master Thumb set out northwards in his quest for the sun. He took with him the cake, which was many times bigger than himself.	Event 10. Counteraction Event 11. Departure Event 14. Receipt of a magical object
It was midsummer, the fields were bare of vegetation, and the whole countryside groaned under the intense heat. As he travelled on, Master Thumb met an old boat that was left high and dry. The stream on which it was floating had been dried up by the sun. 'Master Thumb', greeted the boat, 'where are you going?'	Move 2 Transfer connective Event 15. Guidance
'I go to fight my enemy, the sun', was the reply.	
Now the boat was also very bitter against the sun, for the sun had dried up his stream. So he pleaded, 'Please let me follow you'.	
'All right', replied Master Thumb. 'Eat a bit of my cake and get inside my stomach'. The boat did as he was told.	

(*continued on next page*)

(continued)

'How Master Thumb Defeated the Sun?'[7]	Events
Master Thumb travelled on, and he met a bamboo thorn. 'Where are you going, Master Thumb?' greeted the bamboo thorn.	Event 15. Guidance
'I go to fight my enemy, the sun,' was the reply.	
Now the bamboo thorn also hated the sun, for the sun had caused all the bamboo plants to wither and fade. So he pleaded, 'May I follow you?'	
'All right,' replied Master Thumb. 'Eat a bit of my cake, and get inside my stomach'. The bamboo thorn did as he was told.	
Master Thumb travelled on, and he met a strip of moss. 'Where are you going, Master Thumb?' greeted the moss.	Event 15. Guidance
'I go to fight my enemy, the sun', was the reply.	
Now the moss also hated the sun, for the sun had dried up all the other moss nearby. And this moss had survived only because he had hidden himself among the roots of a big tree. So he pleaded, 'May I come with you?'	
'All right', replied Master Thumb. 'Eat a bit of my cake, and get inside my stomach'. The moss did as he was told.	
Master Thumb travelled on, and he met a rotten egg. 'Where are you going, Master Thumb?' greeted the rotten egg.	Event 15. Guidance
'I go to fight my enemy, the sun', was the reply.	
Now the rotten egg also hated the sun, for his parents and relations, the fowls, had died of thirst as their streams were dried up by the sun. So he pleaded, 'May I come with you?'	
'All right', replied Master Thumb. 'Eat a bit of my cake, and get inside my stomach'. The rotten egg did as he was told.	

(continued on next page)

(continued)

'How Master Thumb Defeated the Sun?'[7]	Events
So our Master Thumb, with his four faithful followers inside his stomach, travelled on until he reached the northern mountains at nightfall, where he expected the sun to appear the next morning.	Move 3 Transfer connective
He decided to rest there for the night and looked around for some shelter. To his surprise, he saw a house some distance away. Master Thumb, being not only courageous but wise, realized that the house could not belong to a human being but to an ogre, for only ogres live on bleak mountains and in wild forests. He walked to the house and decided that it was empty. 'But the owner will come to sleep here for the night', said Master Thumb to himself, 'and so I will wait and fight him for the house. I must have a good night's rest before my big battle'.	Event 4. Reconnaissance
At this moment, the bamboo thorn, the moss, and the rotten egg jumped out of his stomach. 'Master', they pleaded, 'allow us to fight the ogre, for you must reserve your strength for the morrow'. Master Thumb reluctantly agreed and, hiding himself behind a bush, awaited events.	
The three faithful followers entered the house, and the first thing they did was to hide the tinderbox. Then the bamboo thorn placed himself underneath the bed, the rotten egg in the kitchen fireplace, and the moss near the water jar.	Event 6. Trickery
Soon afterwards, a big ogre came in and threw himself on the bed. The bamboo thorn gave him a series of sharp pricks. 'Too many bugs in the bed', the ogre grumbled. 'I must light my lamp and look for them'.	Event 7. Complicity

(continued on next page)

(*continued*)

'How Master Thumb Defeated the Sun?'[7]	Events
He got up and felt for the tinderbox and, not finding it, he went to the kitchen to get a light. But as he bent over the fire the rotten egg burst its shell with a loud bang, scattering the ashes into the ogre's big eyes. The ogre groped his way to the water jar with the intention of washing out the cinders from his eyes, but he slipped on the moss and fell, breaking his neck. The three faithful servants reported the death of the ogre to Master Thumb and placed the house at his disposal.	Event 18. Victory (over villain 2)
At dawn, Master Thumb, with his three faithful followers arrayed beside him, challenged the sun to come out and fight. The sun appeared, red with anger, and as he rose in the sky he made himself hotter and hotter until poor Master Thumb was nearly shrivelled up by the heat. No doubt he would have been ignominiously destroyed had not an unexpected ally come to his aid. Now the rain had been fighting the sun since the beginning of time, and the rain considered anyone who fought the sun worthy of his support. So the rain came down and quenched the sun.	Move 4 Transfer connective Event 16. Struggle (with villain 1) Event 15. Guidance
Master Thumb and his three faithful followers laughed loudly at the sun's discomfort, but soon they became silent with dismay. For the rain, in quenching the sun, had caused great floods and Master Thumb was now in danger of drowning.	***False guidance
At this juncture, however, out jumped the boat from inside Master Thumb's stomach and placed himself at his master's service. Master Thumb and his other followers jumped into the boat and journeyed southwards together back to Master Thumb's village.	Event 15. Guidance Event 18. Victory
All the villagers came out with laughter and with shouts to greet the return of their hero and to celebrate the defeat of the sun.	Event 27. Recognition

The following tales have storylines with the functional events for the fairy tale model.

Tale 6:	'How Master Thumb Defeated the Sun?'
Tale 9:	'The Big Tortoise'
Tale 22	'The Egg-Born King'
Tale 24	'The Hundred and One Lobsters'
Tale 25	'The Snail Prince'
Tale 26	'Khun San Law and Nan Oo Pyin'
Tale 27	'The Origin of the Rainy Season'

The functional events in Tales 22, 24, 25, 26, and 27 are listed in table 7. The summaries of these tales can be found in appendix C. In addition to heroic fairy tales, which are similar to Russian fairy tales, there are some female-centred fairy tales, similar to those studied by Dan (1977), in which the main character is a female protagonist who is subjected to villainy before she is saved by the helper or the donor. Tale 9, 'The Big Tortoise', is an example of the female fairy tale. Because it is made up of six moves and is relatively long, the detailed analysis of its functional events is given in appendix B. The analysis of tales with a fairy tale model has shown that some of the Burmese folk tales are made up of functional events that are similar to those of Russian fairy tales. However, it does not support one of Propp's claims that the sequences of these functional events are always identical.

4.2.6. Tales With a Hybrid Structure

There are also some tales that can be called 'hybrid', in other words, their structures comprise various patterns of functional events and combination sequences. Tale 19, 'The Sun, the Moon, and the Evening Star', is an example of a tale with a hybrid structure.

Table 7. Functional events (E) in the tales with fairy tale model.

Tale no. 22 ***The Egg-Born King***	**Tale no. 24** ***The Hundred and One Lobsters***	**Tale no. 25** ***The Snail Prince***	**Tale no. 26** ***Khun San Law and Nan Oo Pyin***	**Tale no. 27** ***The Origin of the Rainy Season***
Move 1 Information connective 8a. Lack 9. Mediation 11. Departure Transfer connective 12. First function of the donor 13. Receipt of a magical object Move 2 Transition in Space 15.Guidance 16. Struggle 17. Victory 31. Wedding	Move 1 Information connective 5. Delivery 8. Villainy 22. Rescue Move 2 Transition in Time 4. Reconnaissance 5. Delivery 6. Trickery 7. Complicity 8. Villainy 22. Rescue (The same pattern as Move 2 recurs for Moves 3, 4, 5, & 6)	Move 1 Information connective 8a. Lack (1) 11. Departure 15. Guidance Move 2 Transition in Time and Space 8a. Lack (2) 9. Mediation 11. Counteraction 12. Receipt of a magical object 11. Departure Move 3 Transition in Space 15. Guidance 17. Branding 19. Liquidation of (Lack 2)	Move 1 Information connective 1. Absence Transition in Time 8a. Lack 11. Departure Transition in Space 15. Guidance 17. Branding 30. Wedding Move 2 Transition in Space 20. Protagonist's Return 5. Delivery 6. Trickery 7. Complicity 8. Villainy	Move 1 Information connective 1. Absence 8. Villainy 8a. Lack 15. Guidance 19. Liquidation Move 2 Transition in Time 4. Reconnaissance 5. Delivery 6. Trickery 7. Complicity 8. Villainy Move 3 Transition in the State of the Helper 15. Guidance 22. Rescue 30. Wedding

(*continued on next page*)

TABLE 7. *(continued)*

Tale no. 22 ***The Egg-Born King***	**Tale no. 24** ***The Hundred and One Lobsters***	**Tale no. 25** ***The Snail Prince***	**Tale no. 26** ***Khun San Law and Nan Oo Pyin***	**Tale no. 27** ***The Origin of the Rainy Season***
<u>Move 3</u> Transition in Time Information connective 8a. Lack 9. Mediation 17. Branding	<u>Move 7</u> Transition in Time and State of the Protagonists 14. Receipt of a magical object 15. Guidance 16. Struggle 18. Victory 28. Exposure 27. Recognition	<u>Move 4</u> Transition in Time 25. Difficult task 26. Solution 27. Recognition 29.Transfiguration 19. Liquidation of (Lack 1)	<u>Move 3</u> Transition in Time 23. Unrecognised arrival of Protagonist 6. Trickery 7. Complicity 8. Villainy <u>Move 4</u> Transition in Time 28. Exposure 8. New villainy 8a.Lack (Tragedy)	<u>Move 4</u> Transition in Time 20. Return 6. Trickery 28. Exposure 30. Punishment

Note. See table 2 (pp. 34–36) for the explanation of each functional event.

The distribution of characters for the narrative roles and the functional events in Tale 19 are identified as follows:

Protagonist A: The Eldest Daughter
Protagonist B: The Second Daughter
Protagonist C: The Youngest Daughter
Villain: The Old Tiger
Helper: The Rain God

Move 1

Information connective	Protagonists are introduced.
Event 1	Absence The mother went away to attend a sacrificial feast at another village.
Event 2	Interdiction The mother told the three daughters to keep the doors and the windows shut because there was an old tiger that wanted to eat them up.
Transfer connective	Transition in time (days passed).
Event 3	Trickery The old tiger pretended to be the mother and knocked at the door. The tiger asked them to open the door.
Event 4b	Counteraction The eldest daughter, who was on watch that night, asked why her voice was so hoarse and squeaky.
Event 5b	Competition

	The tiger told them that the hoarse and squeaky voice was because of the dancing and singing at the feast. But the daughters were not convinced.
Event 6b	Victory (of the Protagonists)
	The tiger went away.
Event 3	Trickery
	The old tiger came and knocked at the door again, pretending to be the mother.
Event 4b	Counteraction
	The second daughter, who was on watch duty that night, asked the tiger to let them feel its palm.
Event 5b	Competition/struggle
	The daughters felt the palm of the tiger's hand, and asked why it was rough and chapped. The tiger said it was because of all the hard work at the feast. The daughters were not convinced.
Event 6b	Victory (of the Protagonists)
	The old tiger went away.
Event 3	Trickery
	The tiger, pretending to be the mother, came and knocked at the door again.
Event 4a	Submission
	The youngest and kindhearted daughter was on watch duty that night. She did not suspect anything.
Event 5a	Complicity
	She threw open the door.

Event 6a	Victory (of the Villain) The tiger chased the three daughters, who ran to the walnut tree.
Transfer connective	Transition in space. The three daughters were in the walnut tree.

Move 2

Event 3	Trickery The tiger wrapped a blanket around the body and ran to the walnut tree. It pretended to be the mother and asked the three daughters to pull it up the tree.
Event 4b	Counteraction The daughters gave false instructions for climbing up the tree.
Event 5b	Competition/struggle The tiger followed the false instructions and was unsuccessful in climbing up the tree.
Event 4a	Submission The youngest daughter was convinced that it was their mother. She felt sorry for the tiger and give the right instructions to climb up the tree.
Event 5a	Complicity The tiger climbed higher and higher up the tree. The three daughters also climbed higher and higher up the tree.
Event 9	Rescue

	The daughters called out to the rain god to save them. The rain god rescued them by pulling them up in a bucket.
Event 11	Punishment
	The tiger fell into the ocean and drowned as he tried to follow the daughters.
Transfer connective	Transition in space (the three daughters reached the sky).
Event 12	Protagonists returns service to the helper.
	In appreciation, they helped the rain god to watch over the world below—the eldest daughter served as the sun, the second as the moon, and the youngest as the evening star.

As shown in the analysis, the storyline in Tale 19 starts with some functional events of a fairy tale model, such as absence and interdiction. However, as the story progresses, it follows the structure of a trickster tale—'Trickery → Counteraction/ Submission → Competition/Complicity → Victory'. Then the storyline goes on with functional events of a fairy tale model, such as rescue and punishment. It ends with an additional functional event, which is not covered in Propp's model—'Protagonist returns service to the helper'.

Similarly, Tale 4, 'The Four Drums of Destiny', is different in its structure from any of the models. The following is the distribution of characters to the narrative roles in this tale.

Tale 4: 'The Four Drums of Destiny'

Protagonist A: The Eldest Son (The First Brother)
Protagonist B: The Second Son (The Second Brother)

Protagonist C: The Third Son (The Third Brother)
Protagonist D: The Youngest Son (The Fourth Brother)
Donor: The Old Magician (The Father)

The storyline in this tale starts with Propp's functional event 14, receipt of a magical object by the four protagonists from the donor.

Event 14	Receipt of a magical object The old magician father gave a golden drum to the eldest son, a silver drum to the second son, a brass drum to the third son and a tin drum to the youngest son.
Event 1	Absence The old magician father passed away.
Event 8a	Lack The first, second, and third brothers won a kingdom each with the help of their golden, silver, and brass magic drums. But only nymphs and demons came out from the fourth brother's tin drum. So, the fourth brother lived with nymphs and demons in the forest.

The tale is then made up of several additional functional events, such as:

Event ***	Protagonists attempt to equate lack in one of the protagonists. The first, second, and third brothers, in turn, sent heralds to fetch the youngest brother from the forest. Each of them offered the youngest

brother half of their kingdom and made him the crown prince.

Event*** Lack remains and Protagonists in their original states.

Each time after staying in a kingdom for a few months, the youngest brother asked his brothers to let him return to the forest because he found the soldiers in the kingdom too fierce and the treasurers too proud. The youngest brother returned to the forest and lived there forever in the company of nymphs and demons.

4.3. THE DEGREE OF LINEARITY

For an analysis of narrative structures in folk tales, the identification of functional events and the classification of them into different models have to be complemented with the investigation of their interconnectedness and sequentiality in each model. In this section, the linearity—the ways in which these functional events are linked into well-organised storylines in different types of folk tales—will be examined.

As discussed in chapter 2, linearity is one form of narrative dimension, suggested by Ochs and Capps (2001), to find out the extent to which the events in a storyline are linked into a single, closed, temporal, and causal path. The functional events making up different structural patterns in Burmese folk tales, as classified in the previous sections, are found to be threaded into a timeline and cause-effect progression in various ways. The linkage between the functional events in each model can be analysed as follows.

4.3.1. Reward/Punishment Model

	Events (Move 1)	*Linkage*
1.	Guide leads Protagonist A to Donor.	
		Temporal
2.	Protagonist A meets Donor.	
		Temporal
3.	Donor sets Protagonist A tasks/tests.	
		Temporal
4.	Protagonist A performs successfully.	
		Causal
5.	Protagonist A is rewarded.	
	Moves are linked with information and transfer connectives.	
	Events (Move 2)	*Linkage*
6.	Guide leads Protagonist B to Donor.	
		Temporal
7.	Protagonist B meets Donor.	
		Temporal
8.	Donor sets Protagonist B tasks/tests.	
		Temporal
9.	Protagonist B fails.	
		Causal
10.	Protagonist B is punished. (Protagonist B is not rewarded.)	

Thus, the functional events in a move are found to be connected by some co-occurrence rules. That is to say, each functional event anticipates or causes the following one, and each following functional event assumes the existence of the preceding one. In places where the causal relation prevails, the linkage demands the agreement of causality between these two functional events. The positive effect will follow the positive cause, while the negative effect will follow the negative cause.

Sequence of Events	*Causality*
Task → Success → Reward	Positive
Task → Failure→ Punishment	Negative

4.3.2. Interdiction/Violation Model

A similar closed causal path is found in the linkage between the functional events of the interdiction/violation model.

	Events	*Linkage*
1.	Equilibrium or friendship between the protagonists.	
		Temporal/ Causal
2.	An interdiction is made between Protagonist A and Protagonist B.	
		Temporal
3.	Protagonist B is tested.	
		Temporal
4a.	Interdiction is kept.	
		Causal
5a.	Equilibrium or friendship is maintained.	
	(or)	
4b.	Interdiction is violated.	
		Causal

5b. Discovery of violation, the end of equilibrium or friendship.

Sequence of Events	*Causality*
Interdiction → Preservation → Equilibrium maintained	Positive
Interdiction → Violation → Disequilibrium	Negative

4.3.3. Trickster Tales

Similarly, the linkage of functional events in a trickster tale can be illustrated as follows:

Events	*Linkage*
1. Lack or insufficiency in one of the protagonists.	
	Temporal/ Causal
2. One protagonist meets Helper.	
	Temporal/ Causal
3. One protagonist attempts to harm the other with trickery.	
	Temporal
4a. The other protagonist submits to trickery.	
	Causal
5a. The other protagonist complies with the deceitful persuasions.	
	Temporal/ Causal

6a. The victory of the protagonist who plays the trick.	
(or)	
4b. The other protagonist reacts (with another trickery).	
	Causal
5b. Two protagonists are in competition.	
	Temporal/ Causal
6b. The victory of the protagonist who reacts.	
	Causal
7. Resolution	

Sequence of Events	*Causality*
Trickery → Submission → Complicity → Victory of the protagonist who plays the trick.	Positive
Trickery → Counteraction → Competition → Failure of the protagonist who plays the trick.	Negative

4.3.4. Problem/Solution Model

For the problem/solution model, the interconnectedness between the functional events constituting the elementary storyline can be outlined as follows:

Events	*Linkage*
1. Protagonist A meets Protagonist B.	
	Temporal
2. Protagonist A and Protagonist B are in dispute over an object.	
	Causal

3. Protagonist A and Protagonist B meet Guide.

Temporal

4. Guide fails to settle the dispute.

Causal

5. Protagonists meet Helper.

Temporal

6. Helper makes a decision.

4.3.5. Fairy Tales

The classification of functional events, according to their structural similarities, has highlighted the fact that in the case of tales which follow the fairy tale model, the sequence of functional events is not always identical for each tale. Various functional events in each tale are found to be connected by their own sequential meaning. They are found to be organised into moves as members of an ordered set. For example, the linkage of the functional events in Tale 6, 'How Master Thumb Defeated the Sun?', are noted as:

Moves	*Events*	*Linkage*
1	8. a Lack (unusually small size of hero Protagonist)	
		Temporal
	9. Mediation (its cause is made known)	
		Causal
	10. Counteraction (Protagonist decides to fight with Villain who causes the lack)	
		Temporal

	11. Departure (Protagonist leaves home in search of Villain.)	
		Temporal
	14. Receipt of a magical object	

Moves 1 and 2 are linked by a transfer connective—transition in time and space.

Moves	*Events*	*Linkage*
2	15. Guidance (Protagonist meets a helper.)	
		Temporal
	15. Guidance (Protagonist meets another helper.)	
		Temporal
	15. Guidance (Protagonist meets another helper.)	
		Temporal
	15. Guidance (Protagonist meets another helper.)	

Move 2 and Move 3 are linked with a transfer connective—transition in space.

Moves	*Events*	*Linkage*
3	4. Reconnaissance (Protagonist makes reconnaissance of Villain 2.)	
		Temporal

	6. Trickery (Helpers attempt to deceive Villain 2.)	
		Temporal
	7. Complicity (Villain submits to trickery.)	
		Temporal/ Causal
	18. Victory (Helpers defeat Villain 2.)	

Move 3 and Move 4 are linked with a transfer connective—transition in time.

Moves	*Events*	*Linkage*
4	16. Struggle (Protagonist and Villain 1 in competition.)	
		Temporal
	15. Guidance (Protagonist is helped by the helper.)	
		Temporal/ Causal
	***False guidance (Protagonist in danger.)	
		Temporal/ Causal

15. Guidance
    (Protagonist is helped by other helpers.)

Causal

18. Victory
    (Protagonist and helpers defeat Villain.)

Causal

27. Recognition
    (Protagonist is recognised for his victory.)

It is found that a functional event stands in a temporal or causal relation in both directions: towards the functional event that precedes it and one that follows it. Such highly linear narrative structure is described by Ochs and Capps (2001) as a linkage by the sequential meaning, 'the meaning of a narrated event derives in part from its position in a particular temporal sequence' (p. 168).

Event n ← → Event n+1 ← → Event n+2

The temporal and/or causal linkage between each of the two functional events explains the ways in which functional events are connected in a highly linear plot structure, although their sequence of occurrence is not identical in every tale.

4.4. Deviation From a Familiar Trajectory

The analysis of linearity between functional events reveals some storylines that deviate from a familiar unilinear time-line or cause-effect progression. Such deviation from a closed temporal or causal path is found to produce an effect of humour in some tales (e.g., Tale 12, 'How the Opium Eater Went to Heaven?'). The functional events in Tale 12 have been identified in 4.2.4 (pp. 67–69). An instance of deviation from a closed temporal or causal path that produces an effect of humour in this tale can be explained by examining the linkage between its functional events.

Events (Move 1)	*Linkage*
1. Lack or insufficiency in Protagonist A. The opium eater had no record for a great deed of merit to convince the lord judge that he should not be sent to hell.	
	Causal
3. Protagonist A attempts to deceive Protagonist B with trickery. The opium eater told the lord judge that he did *bushein.* The opium eater was using the spoonerism for *beinshu*, which means 'smoke opium' in Burmese.	
	Temporal
4a. Protagonist B submits to trickery. The lord judge thought *bushein* was a term in Pali, the classical language of Buddhism he was not very good at.	
	Causal
5a. Protagonist B complies with the deceitful persuasions.	

The lord judge thought that it must be an important deed of merit to have a Pali reference, and he told the guard to put the opium eater on the middle tier of the chariot to be sent to heaven while he would go and ask the king of gods for advice.

Temporal/ Causal

6a. The victory of the Protagonist who plays the trick.

The guard put the opium eater on the middle tier of the chariot.

Moves 1 and 2 are linked with a transfer connective—transition in time and space.

Events (Move 2)	*Linkage*

3. Protagonist A attempts to harm Protagonist C with trickery.

The opium eater told the old man sitting on the lower tier of the chariot that the old man, for being a very considerate person with charming manners, deserved to be on the middle tier.

Temporal

4a. Protagonist C submits to trickery.

The old man was convinced that the lord judge must have misjudged the nature of his deeds of merit.

Causal

5a. Protagonist C complies with the deceitful persuasions.

The old man agreed to change seats with the opium eater.

Temporal/ Causal

6a. The victory of Protagonist A.

The opium eater managed to change his seat to the lower tier before the lord judge returned from the king of gods.

Off temporal path (Move 1 continued)

7. Resolution (Discovery of the trickery)

The lord judge found out from the king of gods about the spoonerism.

Causal(?)

4b. Protagonist B reacts.

The lord judge angrily pulled down the person sitting on the middle tier of the chariot and threw him into hell.

Temporal

6a. The victory of Protagonist A, who plays the trick.

The opium eater, who had moved to the lower tier of the chariot, was carried to heaven.

As noted in the analysis of functional events and their linkage, Protagonist A still succeeds in spite of Protagonist B's reaction. Protagonist B's discovery of Protagonist A's trick comes only *after* a transition in time and space (i.e., only after Protagonist A has successfully transferred himself to a new place). Thus, the functional event (7) resolution fails to follow the right temporal path. This off-temporal path leads to the success of Protagonist A, who is not supposed to escape punishment from the point of view of a moral lesson.

Similarly, in Tale 14, 'The Four Deaf Men', the storyline seems to be following the first part of the problem/solution model. However, the dispute in the tale is not over an object, but because of the misunderstanding among the four deaf men. Protagonists are misled into a dispute that is later accidentally solved by the helper. The unusual causal relationship between its functional events is the element that causes humour in the tale.

Tale 14: 'The Four Deaf Men'

Distribution of characters in narrative roles:

Protagonist A: The Herdsman
Protagonist B: The Toddy-Climber
Protagonist C: The Farmer
Helper: The Headman

'The Four Deaf Men'[8]	**Events**
Once there lived four deaf men in a village. The first was a herdsman, the second earned his living by climbing palm trees to extract toddy juice, the third was a farmer, and the fourth the headman of the village.	<u>Move 1</u> Information connective—Protagonists are introduced.

(*continued on next page*)

(continued)

'The Four Deaf Men'[8]	Events
One morning, the herdsman missed his cattle, which had strayed away during the night. He searched and searched but without success. Then he saw the toddy climber up a palm tree and asked, 'Have you seen my cattle?'	Event 1. Lack in Protagonist A. (Protagonist A has a problem.) Event 2. Protagonist A meets Protagonist B.
The toddy climber, of course, could not hear him, but thought the herdsman was asking about the palms. 'This tree is not so good', he said, and he pointed to a grove some distance away. 'The trees over there are much better'.	Event 3. False Guidance
'Thank you', said the herdsman, thinking that the toddy climber was telling him where to find the missing cattle. He went to the distant grove of palm trees and actually found his cattle there.	<u>Unusual causal linkage</u> Event 4. Lack is liquidated. (Problem is solved.)
The herdsman was now hot and tired from searching for his cattle the whole morning, and he wanted to take the shortcut to his home. To do that, he had to go over the land belonging to the farmer. The herdsman found the farmer burning the meadow grass on his land and, pointing to his cattle, he said, 'May I cross with my cattle?'	<u>Move 2</u> Event 5. Lack in Protagonist A. Event 6. Protagonist A meets Protagonist C.
The farmer thought that the question was 'Did you steal my cattle?' and he replied, 'No, no', shaking his head vigorously.	Event 7. False Guidance
'Now, now', said the herdsman, 'why are you so mean? Your land is not yet plowed, and surely my cattle cannot spoil it'.	Event 8. Protagonist A and Protagonist C are in dispute.
The farmer went on shaking his head, saying 'No, no'. At last they came to blows and each dragged the other to the headman's house.	Event 9. Protagonists meet Helper.
The headman that morning had had an unfortunate misunderstanding with his wife, which resulted in his soundly beating her. The wife left the house in disgust and went home to her mother. The herdsman and the farmer	

(continued on next page)

(*continued*)

'The Four Deaf Men'[8]	Events
arrived, each sued the other for assault, and each pleaded his case with eloquent gestures.	
But the headman shook his head, and waving his hands, he said, 'Go away! Go away! It is no good pleading on her behalf. I will not have her back. Let her stay on with her mother'.	Event 10. False Guidance
The herdsman and the farmer, believing that both their suits had been dismissed, went away quietly.	Unusual causal linkage Event 11. Problem is solved.

It is also noted that in some cases, a unique sequence of functional events may be the reflection of a different subtype of tales. For example, the storyline of Tale 26, 'Khun San Law and Nan Oo Pyin' (pp. 77–78), is found to end with 'Lack', a functional event that normally takes place at the beginning of a tale or in relation to the start of a new move. This gives the tale a sad ending and some likeness to a tragedy in which the two protagonists who are lovers are separated forever.

CHAPTER 5

EVENTS, MOVES, AND THE STORYLINE

Through the analysis of functional events in different types of tales and their linkage in each pattern, some narrative structures of Burmese folk tales have been presented in various models. In this chapter, the findings from the analysis will be discussed in terms of events, moves, and the storyline.

5.1. FUNCTIONAL EVENTS AS THE FUNDAMENTAL UNITS

It is found that in folk tales, and not just in the fairy tales upon which Propp's (1968) study was based, actions are of greater consequence and of higher relevance for the structure of a tale than the dramatis personae who carry out these actions. When regarded with caution, Propp's concept of functional events is still found to be applicable to the structural analysis of tales with various themes or from a different culture.

At the same time, event alone has proved to be insufficient for a description of narrative structures in folk tales. Other units, such as moves and connectives, have to be considered, in order to describe how these fundamental events are 'knitted' into an overarching storyline, with a high degree of linearity in its plot structure. Propp assumed the high degree of linearity among the functional events identified in his study, when he claimed that the sequence of the functional events is always identical. However, the functional events and combination sequences identified in the present study do not support this claim because they are not found to be identical in all types of tales.

Only when the structure of a tale follows one of these models—reward/punishment, interdiction/violation, problem/solution, or trickster tale—are its constituting functional events and their combination sequences found to be identical or similar to that of the elementary storyline for each model. Conversely, the fairy tale model is found to comprise functional events whose combination sequences are unique for each tale.

The analysis of functional events in Burmese folk tales also raises some questions on grouping these events into binary pairs. Based on the findings in his study, Propp (1968) stated that 'a large number of functions are arranged in pairs' (p. 64). Accordingly, he outlined the combination of events in binary pairs as follows (Propp, 1968, pp. 64–65):

lack	–	lack liquidated
interdiction/prohibition	–	violation
reconnaissance	–	delivery
attempt at deceit	–	act of being deceived

test	–	receipt of magical agent
struggle/contest	–	victory
pursuit	–	deliverance

These binary pairs represent only one possible causal path. It has been illustrated in the analysis that the functional events in a model can be summarised into two parallel patterns instead of one binary pair. They can follow either a positive or negative causal path, resulting in a different follow-up functional event.

Lack → Guidance → Lack liquidated
→ False guidance → Lack remains

Interdiction → Preservation → Equilibrium maintained
→ Violation → Disequilibrium

Trickery → Submission → Complicity → Victory of the Protagonist who plays the trick
→ Counteraction → Competition → Victory of the Protagonist who reacts

Task → Success → Reward
→ Failure → Punishment

Highlighting the existence of alternative possibilities, the present study has made a refinement on Propp's linear sequence. Propp's definition of lack as the only one absolutely necessary functional event in the structure of a tale has also been broadened. By identifying the functional events forming various structural patterns and by summarising them into elementary storylines of each model, this study has tried to specify certain functional events as the minimum number of connecting links or the fundamental constituents of that model.

Moreover, the analysis of folk tales in this study has also pointed out that the lack is not a necessary functional event to begin a storyline, and in most cases, lack is implied rather than evident. It is also possible for a tale to end with the functional event of lack, creating a sad ending or in some cases producing an effect of humour.

Another interesting finding in this study is that the functional event serving as dénouement in Burmese folk tales are not restricted to a particular event of wedding as in the Russian fairy tales. The endings of the folk tales vary from one another, in contrast to the morally edifying wonder tales, which are governed by the optimistic requirement of a happy ending.

The findings in this study can therefore justify the claim that the functional event lack is not always evident for the development of a tale, and that other events, other than a wedding, are more common as a conclusion in Burmese folk tales. It is also recognised that although functional events serve as the fundamental constituents in the narrative structures of these tales, their combination into a basic storyline may vary, creating different types of structural patterns.

The fact that constituting functional events and their combination sequences may not be identical in each and every tale leads to the need to discuss the possible ways in which the events are grouped into moves, which are in turn combined into an overarching storyline of the tale as a whole.

5.2. Extension or Embedding of Moves

In the analysis, the linkage between each of the two functional events is explained by investigating their temporal and causal connection. However, the temporal succession and causal connection between functional events are not the only necessary links in the narrative structures of folk tales. They are not in themselves sufficient to explain the plot structure of those tales consisting of various moves. Each model discovered in the analysis represents only a series of functional events, a move. With variation in the length of the tales, some of the tales comprise only one move, whereas others consist of several moves.

The unit that serves as a link between each of the two successive moves is the connective. It can be one or both types of connectives—information connective and transfer connective (in state, time, or space). These connectives not only help the storyline of a tale become a well-organised narrative, but they also serve as a device through which tales are continued to the end in some cases. For example, the transition in the state of the protagonist from a girl to a paddy bird and then back to a girl in Tale 9, 'The Big Tortoise' (appendix B), enables the narrative to continue to a great length by forming new moves, which are still connected to each other in a linear and coherent storyline.

The moves identified in the analysis of the present study correspond to the description of what Propp labelled as *episodic move*. In its strictest sense, Propp contended that a new move is created by a new act of villainy or lack, which can itself be a tale. This causes some overlap between a move and a tale, and this raises such questions as 'Under what conditions do several moves form a single tale? When are we confronted by two or more tales?' (Propp, 1968, p. 94). Conversely, an episodic move does not necessarily start with a new act of villainy or lack. According to Ochs and Capps (2001), episodes can be understood as 'textual units consisting of an articulated chain of events that cohere around a focal character, topic, or goal' (p. 170).

Because the event lack is not always evident in some models and because a tale does not necessarily begin with that event, a move in the narrative structures of Burmese folk tales can only be defined as an episode or an interpretive frame in which events are put into a temporal and/or causal sequence as members of an ordered set. A new move may introduce new functional events in the same structural pattern as in the reward/punishment model. Alternatively, it may be just the recurrence of the same pattern with the same functional events that are carried out by different characters taking up the narrative roles, as in Tale 1, 'The Cat Who Pretended to Be a University Professor' (pp. 63–65).

It is also noted that moves are combined into a storyline of a tale in two different ways: extension or embedding. The complexity in the narrative structures of Burmese folk tales is found to be a result, more commonly of the extension, and in a few cases, of the embedding of moves. In most of the tales, moves are joined by means of extension—the addition of a new move at the end of the first one. A more complex and less common way is by means of embedding, where a new move begins before the termination of the first one. When the two moves are joined by embedding, the temporal and causal path of the first move is interrupted by a new move. The completion of the first move follows only after the completion of the new move (e.g., Tale 12, 'How the Opium Eater Went to Heaven?' [pp. 93–95]).

Another possible way of combining a new move, which is not found in the analysis, is by means of parallelism, or, in other words, two or more moves progressing in parallel. It is observed from the analysis that even when a tale consists of two protagonists, who stand in contrast to each other or are competing on equal terms, their actions forming the functional events in the structure of the tale are carried out in two successive moves, which are linked by extension, instead of two moves progressing in parallel. The avoidance of paralleled moves has also been commented upon by Bremond (1977) in his study of the morphology of the French fairy tale as a characteristic that 'distinguishes the folktale, a more primitive narrative genre, from more complex genres such as the novel' (p. 65).

5.3. Evaluating the Storyline of a Tale as a Whole

According to Propp (1968),

> Morphologically, a tale may be termed any development proceeding from villainy or a lack, through intermediary functions to marriage, or to other functions employed as a dénouement. (p. 92)

The analysis of the folk tales selected for the present study has, however, highlighted various structural patterns forming different types of tales. It is implied that a single sequence of functional events cannot be claimed as identical for different types of tales. The present study has identified all the constituting functional events in these tales. The study has also illustrated that the temporal and/or the causal relationship of each of the two successive functional events in a pattern must be in agreement for a logical link to occur between them. With the findings on the similarities in the basic storylines of some tales following a model, and the possibilities of deviation from it, an additional issue that has come up for discussion is the criteria to evaluate the storyline of a tale as well organised.

Following Ochs and Capps (2001), a storyline can be regarded as well organised when its plot structure shows a high degree of linearity, in which events are radically correlative, enchaining and entailing. In other words, each functional event is a follow-up to the preceding one and, at the same time, a precursor of the following. 'Relatively linear narratives depict an overarching progression of events in which one event temporally precedes or causally leads to a subsequent event' (Ochs & Capps, 2001, p. 41).

This study has also demonstrated that, when the combination sequence of functional events in a tale is not identical to the basic storyline of a model, Ochs and Capps' concept of sequential meaning (2001) can usefully explain the logical link between each of the two successive functional events. Regardless of the combination sequences that may or may not be identical for every tale, a high degree of linearity between each of the two functional events and between two successive moves will still prove a tale to have a linear and coherent narrative structure.

This principle of agreement in the prevailing causality has to be followed until the closing functional event of a tale. A closing functional event can be proved as an appropriate conclusion of a sequence, when it is the closure of a causal path taken by the preceding functional events. The pragmatic importance of narrative closure is regarded by Leitch (1986) as a factor that 'justifies discursive sequence as whole, complete, and so intelligible as a totality' (p. 43). It is further pointed out by Ochs and Capps (2001) that

> [l]inear, coherent narratives generally have a plot structure that depicts a sequence of temporally and causally ordered events organized around a point, with a beginning...and moves logically towards an ending that provides a sense of psychological closure. (p. 5)

Although not every tale rigidly follows the structure of a model, most are found to approach or are appropriate to the elementary storyline of one of the models. Although events are found to be linked into familiar temporal or causal trajectories in most of the tales, some deviations from these familiar trajectories are also observed.

As noted in the analysis, the deviation in Tales 12 and 14 is made for an effect of humour. Such deviation from an unmarked interpretation is described by Giora (1991) in her study on the cognitive aspects of jokes, in terms of a linear shift, which is one of the conditions necessary for a joke to be well formed. Therefore, some deviations from the familiar trajectories can be explained as a reflection of a different subtype of tales. It reinforces the notion that plot structures are linked to generic forms of story organisation, as claimed by Ochs and Capps (2001) and Swales (1990).

With functional events as well as the relations among them playing an important role in distinguishing the plot structure of a particular form of story organisation, and in analysing narrative structures of a genre, both of them together serve as the criteria in evaluating the storyline of a narrative as well organised. In story grammar research, a well-organised storyline of a tale should be understood as only one source of evidence in evaluating the story grammar as well formed.

Following the concept of sentence grammar, Johnson and Mandler (1980) described the models of the structure of stories as 'story grammar', which outlines the types of information that listeners expect to encounter in a story and the organisation they tend to impose on that information. However, with the findings from their study, they asserted that

> more traditional sources of evidence for evaluation grammars, such as intuitive judgements about well-formedness and constituent structure, must be supplemented with evidence based on the relation of the proposed structures to the details of psychological processing. (Johnson & Mandler, 1980, p. 51)

Their attempts at applying the concepts of observational adequacy and descriptive adequacy, which have been widely used by linguists to assess the 'well-formedness' of sentence grammar, lead to a finding that stories appear to be too complex for listeners to make any but the crudest judgments of 'well-formedness'. Thus, they suggest relying instead on other psychological measures, such as ease of comprehension and recall of stories, in order to validate a model of story structure as being well or ill formed.

Evaluating the storyline of a tale as a well-organised plot structure, in contrast to 'well-formedness', using linearity as a narrative dimension, as suggested by Ochs and Capps, will save the problems of making such controversial judgments. The closed (or open) temporal and causal order of the constituting functional events, as they are interwoven into a storyline of a tale, can be demonstrated in a continuum, covering a range of possibilities.

One possible problem in evaluating the storyline of a tale as well organised in terms of causal relations among the functional events is the difference in cultural conventions. It can obscure causal connections when a tale is transferred from one culture to another. However, it does not mean that the causal connections do not exist in a tale as it is understood within the original culture. This issue should be further investigated by those who are interested in examining the universality of folk-tale structure and the possible universal models capable of generating narratives in this genre.

Chapter 6

Form, Function, and Field

This chapter will take a closer look at two structural patterns, among others, identified in the earlier chapters. The investigation and descriptions of different structural patterns for various types of folk tales from Burma have highlighted the use of the reward/punishment model and the interdiction/violation model in a number of tales. Thus, this chapter will examine those tales further and explore the possibility of making claims on the relationship between the narrative structure (form), the social purpose (function), and the story content (field) of folk tales.

First, for the discussion of the use of the reward/punishment model, references will be made to the findings from earlier analyses of the narrative structures in Burmese folk tales with a didactic moral purpose. The discussion will also refer to the findings from a recent study done by Grayson (2002) on Korean folk tales with a similar didactic moral purpose.

It is often claimed that in most Asian cultures, folk tales have been preserved for generations not only as a reflection of a particular culture but also as a means of instilling certain concepts in the society (Eugenio, 1995; Grayson, 2002). By looking at the similarities in the use of the reward/punishment model or *contrastive narrative structure* for the didactic purpose in folk tales from Burma (where the culture is mainly based on Theravada Buddhism) and those from Korea (where the culture highlights many Confucian virtues), the discussion in this chapter aims to explore the possibilities of discovering the relationship between the narrative structure (or form of a story) and its function and field. Understanding this relationship among the form, function, and field of folk tales can help to explain the significance of a structural analysis of folk tales, for example, how it can be used as a technique of gaining insights into the cultural determination of the narrative motif and the social purpose of storytelling.

6.1. Form, Function, and Field of a Tale

Form, *function*, and *field* have been claimed as the three major criteria in the classification of a genre (Swales, 1990). In this perspective, the form of a tale can be defined as its narrative structure, the function as its social purpose, and the field as its content. Tracing back the literature on the studies of tales, it is found that most of the classifications of tales in a collection are based on the narrative motif or the content of the stories (e.g., animal tales, fairy tales, trickster tales, phenomenon tales, wonder tales, etc.). However, as pointed out by Martin (1986), such thematic categorisations on the basis of a tale's subject matter or content, can lead to some problems due to the inconsistency in the choice of criterion. It can be argued that the theme of an animal tale can be the same as those of a wonder tale and that animals can be taking the narrative roles in a wonder tale.

Conversely, classifications of tales based on a structural analysis are not exempted from disapproving comments as well. As discussed in chapter 2, the structural analysis of tales can be claimed to have begun with Propp's (1968) groundbreaking morphological classification of Russian folk tales. Following Propp, scholars such as Dundes (1965, 1971) and Bremond (1977) studied the structures of folk tales from various cultures. Dundes (1965) studied the structural typology of North American Indian folk tales and proposed a formal analysis of tales as a means to gain an understanding of concrete human behaviour and thought. In his study on African folk tales, Dundes (1971) illuminated how the making and breaking of friendship serves as a structural frame within which a variety of tale types occur in that culture. Similarly, Bremond (1977) attempted to construct a formal model for analysing and classifying the episodes of the fairy tale and also proposed the morphology of French fairy tales.

These studies illustrated the significance and use of structural analyses not only for making typological statements but also for understanding the cultural determination of contents within possibly transcultural forms. In fact, the foregrounding of a sequence of events in these studies has contributed to many interesting story grammars (de Beaugrande, 1982) and has also led to the heyday of narrative structure studies under the term narratology (Genette, 1980).

However, with the growing interest in narrative as a social and psychological phenomenon, rather than solely as a formal literary or historical genre, the theories and practices in the structural analyses of stories came under attack (Rimmon-Kenan, 2002) and are often accused of disregarding the content in the search for the form. Martin (1986) contended that although the explorations of story structures using different methods have resulted in various descriptions of different models, what is lacking in most of the models is an explanation of how formal patterns are related to the story's content. Thus, poststructuralist studies of stories have tried to include the other two aspects of the genre—the function and the field—in specifying and explaining the nature of stories.

For example, in understanding a story on the basis of its function or social purpose, Brewer and Lichtenstein (1982) took a narrower view and claimed that '*stories are a subclass of narratives which have entertainment as their primary discourse force*' (p. 478, emphasis in original). However, as pointed out by Stein (1982), such claims overlook the multifaceted nature of a story because the social purposes of different types of stories vary. There should be no doubt about a large number of stories that carry other functions beyond entertainment. Stories can work to resolve personal social problems and to recapitulate and reorganise personal experience (Labov & Waletzky, 1967); to establish social identity, social relationship, social hierarchies, and emotional bonds (Bloome, 2003); to educate, persuade, warn, reassure, justify, explain, and console members of an organisation (Gabriel, 2000), among others.

In the case of folk tales, it can generally be accepted that the function or the social purpose of storytelling is to preserve the culture of a civilization, to explain natural phenomena, to transmit historical and important social information, or to teach important moral and ethical issues (Taylor, 2000). With the culturally determined setting for such folkloristic storytelling, it can also be argued that there is thematic restriction of the subject matters in folk tales (Fludernik, 1996).

As discussed earlier, what is at issue in a study of folk tales in particular, and of stories in general, is how the structural features of a story can be related to its contents and functions. Therefore, the form, function, and field of those tales that have the structural pattern of the reward/punishment model and those with the interdiction/violation model will be examined further to find out how the narrative structure of a tale complements (and is in turn complemented by) its educational or social function of insinuating psychologically significant themes or contents. First, some explanation is given on the term *contrastive narrative structure*. To illustrate, a Burmese folk tale (Tale 7, 'The Golden Crow') analysed in chapter 4 for its narrative structure, will be used as the sample text.

6.2. Contrastive Narrative Structure

To recapitulate, for an analysis of the narrative structure in a tale, this study has adopted Propp's (1968) claim that an event—as an act of a character defined from the point of view of its significance for the course of the action—can be extracted as basic components of the tale. The study has also adapted Propp's concept on the distribution of narrative roles to the characters in the tale. Following the classification of characters in the tale to appropriate narrative roles, the functional events constituting the storyline of the tale are identified. Moreover, because a tale may comprise more than one elementary sequence of events, the notions of *move* by Propp (1968) and *connectives* by Jason (1977) have been used to explain the linkage between sequences of functional events. *Move* is a label introduced by Propp for a series of events. Based on Propp's notion of move, Jason (1977) introduced an additional unit, *connective*, for the analysis of narrative structures in oral literature. A connective, which can be either an information connective or a transfer connective in state, time, or space, is a 'unit which connects parts of the narrative' (Jason, 1977, p. 104). The study has regarded such connectives as another type of fundamental constituent, like events, which serve as a device through which tales are arranged into a well-organised storyline.

With events, moves, and connectives as the units of analysis, the basic story structure in Tale 7, 'The Golden Crow', has been outlined as follows:

1. There are two protagonists—one who behaves according to certain specific rules and is rewarded, and the other one who breaks these rules and is punished.
2. The four narrative roles in the tale are distributed as follows:

    a. Protagonist A: Good-Natured Girl
    b. Protagonist B: Bad-Tempered Girl
    c. Donor: Golden Crow
    d. Guide: Tray of Paddy

3. Protagonist A is the main character in the first move of the story, and Protagonist B in the second move. They are comparable and stand in contrast to each other. The Donor role is distributed among several characters who set a test for the protagonists.
4. The narrative structure in this type of tale can be said to comprise 'two symmetrically opposed moves which are formally identical' (Drory, 1977, p. 32). The structure of the sequence of events can be summarised as:
   Tasks → Success → Reward
   Tasks → Failure → Punishment

This kind of story structure, which is composed of two contrasting narrative moves or sections comprising—in turn—a parallel series of scenes, has been discussed in the earlier chapters as the reward/punishment model. Interestingly, a very similar kind of story structure is identified by Grayson (2002) as *contrastive narrative structure* in his study of Korean folk tales. Grayson examined 'The Story of Hungbu and Nolbu' as the best-known Korean example of tales about a good, younger brother and an evil, older brother. The narrative structure of 'The Story of Hungbu and Nolbu' is outlined by Grayson (2002, p. 52) as follows:

Act 1:	The younger brother
Scene 1:	The good actions of the younger brother
Scene 2:	The younger brother's reward
Act 2:	The older brother
Scene 1:	The evil actions of the older brother
Scene 2:	The punishment of the older brother

Following the method used in the present study to analyse the narrative structures of Burmese folk tales, the basic story structure of 'The Story of Hungbu and Nolbu' can be outlined as:

1. There are two protagonists—a kind, generous one who is rewarded for his good actions and a malicious, greedy one who is punished for his bad actions.
2. The four narrative roles in the tale are distributed as follows:

    a. Protagonist A: Hungbu (the kind, generous younger brother)
    b. Protagonist B: Nolbu (the malicious, greedy older brother)

c. Donor: The Young Swallow
d. Guide: Snake

3. Protagonist A (the younger brother) is the main character in the first move of the story. The kind, generous younger brother saved the young swallow from the snake. His kind action to the swallow was rewarded when the large gourds from the plant he grew from the seed dropped by the swallow contained rice and gold, as well as the nymph who helped to build a splendid house for him.
4. Protagonist B (the older brother) is the main character in the second move. The malicious, greedy older brother, after finding out about how his younger brother gained great wealth, broke the swallow's leg before he gave treatment to the injured leg. He was punished for his bad action when the large gourds from the plant he grew from the seed dropped by the swallow brought forth little imps and debt collectors who beat him up, and then a flood of dirty, smelly water deluged his house.
5. The narrative structure in this type of tale can also be found to comprise 'two symmetrically opposed moves which are formally identical'. (Drory, 1977, p. 32)

Similar to Tale 7, 'The Golden Crow'—a Burmese folk tale—the Korean folk tale, 'The Story of Hungbu and Nolbu', is also composed of two equal narrative sections or acts (c.f. moves in the analysis of Burmese folk tales), each consisting of two scenes that balance each other with parallel narrative content but come to a different conclusion, or dénouement. The first act (or Move 1) provides a didactic moral point by showing the good motives and their consequences, whereas the second act (or Move 2), which is formally identical to the first, contrasts the narrative content of the previous act to emphasise the punishment that arises from bad motives.

6.3. Contrastive Narrative Structure and Didactic Moral

The parallel sets of contrasting narratives in the analysis of the tales 'The Golden Crow' and 'The Story of Hungbu and Nolbu' show how good actions are rewarded and evil actions are punished. It outlines one of the primary functions of this particular type of tale—moral teaching. Despite the outwardly simple appearance, tales of this type address themes and issues that are profound for all humanity. It touches on such psychologically significant themes of honesty, kindness, generosity, jealousy, arrogance, greed, and so forth.

In the example of the folk tale from Burma, through the kind actions and modest choices made by Protagonist A and the ways rewards were given for her contentment, the tale appears to be instilling the concept of contentment, a virtue particularly valued in Theravada Buddhism and the Burmese culture. Conversely, through the inhospitable actions and greedy choices made by Protagonist B and the punishment she received for her greed, the tale exposes the negative association of greed. In the teaching of Theravada Buddhism, greed is an element, along with anger and delusion, which is believed to be the root of immoral *kamma* (a Pali word meaning action). Accordingly, greed is an element that one needs to eradicate in the quest to attain *nirvana* (i.e., the state of being free from suffering) in Theravada Buddhism, the religion of the majority of Burmese people.

In similar ways, the example of the Korean folk tales shows how the kind actions are rewarded and the malicious ones are punished; this illustrates how the cultural norms of social assistance are (re)affirmed by the tale and how seriously the violations of cultural norms are treated. However, it is claimed that through the portrayal of how the kind and virtuous younger brother whose generous actions and kind life is rewarded while the greed and maliciousness of the older brother is severely punished, the tale's purpose is not simply to show good is rewarded and evil punished (Grayson, 2002). The tale also reflects certain Confucian values, specifically the social relationships between the elder and younger brothers, which have been embedded in Korean society.

Although a comparison of narrative content in the two tales reveals certain culture-specific elements, for example, the choice of Protagonists (widows and their daughters versus the elder and younger brothers), Donor (a golden crow versus a swallow), and the nature of rewards and punishments, the social purpose of teaching morally significant issues on what is right and its consequences are common in tales from both cultures. Moreover, such morally significant issues are foregrounded in both tales when they are placed in parallel against what is wrong and its consequences. In other words, it appears that the contrastive narrative structure is used commonly in folk tales with a social purpose of teaching morally significant issues in different cultures. Thus, a reasonable claim can be made to point out the relationship between the form (narrative structure), the function (social purpose), and the field (narrative content). The contrastive narrative structure complements and reinforces the moral and ethical messages that lie behind the differing narrative content of folk tales with a similar didactic moral.

Folk tales are typically regarded as children's stories in the modern world. Certainly they do appeal to children and help them in developing critical, social, cognitive, and linguistic skills. At the same time, it should be noted that the themes and issues raised in these tales can be significant to all ages and races.

Although folk tales from different cultures may display many differences, some elements can be justifiably claimed to be common to many or all cultures. Different cultures may offer different tasks or tests for the protagonists, nevertheless, the underlying message of what is morally or ethically right, what is wrong, and the consequences of actions prove to be the same.

Interestingly, aside from the common social and moral themes that lie behind the stories, the reward/punishment model or the contrastive narrative structure is also found to be common for rendering such messages of moral concerns in tales from different cultures. In other words, the relationship of narrative form, function, and field in tales with the didactic moral seems to appear in folk tales from many lands. Just as such moral concerns of honesty, kindness, and generosity—as opposed to jealousy, greed, and pride—are issues in any culture, the contrastive structural form of presenting those issues are also found to be transcultural, if not universal.

To look at other tales with a similar didactic moral from another culture, one can also quote the study by Drory (1977), who has made an attempt to formulate a model for the narrative structure of the reward/punishment fairy tale, such as 'Ali Baba and the Forty Thieves'. Drory contended that the reward-and-punishment fairy tale, with its story structure composed of two symmetrically opposed moves that are formally identical, features two symmetrically opposed protagonists who are tested by the ethical norms. In other words, the actions of the narrative roles are evaluated to some extent in the framework of the socioreligious system of general values and specific norms.

The study by Grayson (2002) on Korean folk tales has also proved that there is a large set of Korean folk tales that are composed of parallel sets of contrasting narratives showing how good actions are rewarded and evil actions punished. Grayson claimed that the contrastive narrative structure can be found in tales throughout East Asia and the world. However, Grayson distinguishes Korean tales from similar tales in China and Japan as an illustration of the Confucian concept of moral suasion or social relationships between brothers, in addition to the common theme of rewards and punishments. According to Grayson, the uniqueness of the Korean tale is its characteristic Confucian subtext (i.e., the emphasis on the moral power of the younger brother to influence his older brother to reform his behaviour). With the role inversion of the protagonist and antagonist, the importance of the value of moral suasion is claimed to be stressed in Korean folk tales. In Grayson's (2002) words:

> However, in this story it is not the elder brother but the younger brother who is the moral teacher. It is this dramatic aspect of the story which is so shocking for the Korean listener and perhaps may account for its immense popularity there. (p. 54)

Regardless of such uniqueness, it can still be argued that these folk tales with a didactic moral from different cultures show the possibility of making claims about the relationship between the contrastive narrative structure, the narrative content of moral issues, and the social function of moral teaching. In other words, it is implied that through the use of a contrastive narrative structure, the virtues of good ethics are emphasised for the purpose of moral teaching in folk tales from different cultures.

6.4. Interdiction/Violation Model and Making/Breaking of Friendship

Another feature that suggests the possibility of relating the form, function, and field of a tale is the narrative structure noted in those tales with the interdiction/violation model. As illustrated in the analysis of narrative structure in Tale 13, 'The Great King Eats Chaff' (pp. 48–49), tales with this model revolve around two protagonists and an interdiction or a contract made between them. Narrative roles are equally distributed between Protagonist A and Protagonist B. Move 1 of the narrative structure portrays the equilibrium and an interdiction or a contract made between the two protagonists. The preservation of the interdiction or contract in the subsequent move(s) will lead to the continuation of equilibrium whereas the violation will result in the end of equilibrium. The narrative structure of those tales with the social purpose of explaining the importance of preserving the interaction in order to maintain the equilibrium can be outlined as:

Interdiction → Preservation → Equilibrium maintained (or)
Interdiction → Violation → Disequilibrium

What is interesting about this model is that a similar narrative structure has been discovered by Dundes (1971) in his studies of African folk tales. Dundes (1971) noted that in the African folk tales with a social purpose of explaining the importance of keeping the contract made between two friends in order to preserve the friendship, the basic narrative structure is:

Friendship
Contract
Violation (e.g., by means of deceit)
Discovery (of violation)
End of friendship

Dundes (1971) concluded that this pattern of the making and breaking of friendship serves as a structural frame for tales with a social function of instilling the significance of friendship in the African culture. His claim is supported by evidence achieved through the comparison of the African folk tales and American Indian folk tales. While the American Indian folk tales do have such events as deceit or deception, the narrative content of friendship is said to be conspicuously absent (Dundes, 1971, p. 180).

The analysis of narrative structures in Burmese folk tales has revealed the use of narrative structure, interdiction/violation model, which is similar to the making/breaking of friendship structural frame discovered by Dundes in his study of African folk tales. However, unlike the African folk tales, the narrative content in Burmese folk tales with this kind of structure is not limited to the friendship and its significance. As illustrated in the analysis of Tale 13 ('The Great King Eats Chaff'), Tale 11 ('Not Angry, but Buffalo Tails Have Become Short' [pp. 51–52]), and Tale 18 ('Why Female Elephants Hate Pregnant Women' [pp. 50–51]), an interdiction or contract can be made between a human and an animal (e.g., the woman and the female elephant), between two members of a family (e.g., the father and the son-in-law), or between a figure of authority and a subject (e.g., the king and the attendant). This feature seems to imply the significance or importance placed on the keeping of the interdiction made with any other members of the society (including those figures of authority and animals) in order to preserve the equilibrium in Burmese culture. Thus, while the study concurs with Dundes (1971) in claiming that narrative structures in folk tales can be multiculturally relative, it is also noted that specific content of tales can be culturally or individually relative.

In summary, a comparison between the two common structural patterns identified in the analysis of Burmese folk tales and those discussed in earlier and recent studies of folk tales from different cultures shows that despite certain culture-specific narrative contents, tales with similar social purposes (e.g., a didactic moral purpose) exhibit similar structural patterns. This finding suggests that certain structural patterns are used commonly (if not universally) by various cultures for the similar social purpose of storytelling. At the same time, the finding also implies that although different cultures may share the same structural pattern, the narrative contents of a tale (e.g., elements taking up the narrative roles) remain culture specific. This has led to several interesting issues, such as the (im)possibilities of finding a universal grammar of folk tales, or at least folk tales from adjacent countries whose cultures are most likely to have influenced the other's.

6.5. A Means to an End

Based on the relationship that exists between the form, function, and field of tales, one of the important implications made by the discussion in this chapter is that an investigation of narrative structures in folk tales can be used as a method to find out the cultural determination of narrative motif and the social purpose of storytelling. For example, in the case of stories with the didactic moral, the contrastive narrative structure serves as reinforcement in instilling the concepts of good morals, which are profound and significant for all humanity across various cultures. The feasibility to examine the relationship of narrative form, function, and field in other types of stories, nevertheless, is left open for further explorations.

The discussion in this chapter also implies that for a better understanding of the nature and the power of stories, it is useful to probe the relationship among the underlying story structures, the narrative contents presented, and the social functions of storytelling in various types of stories. In a poststructural, postmodern world, the structural analysis of stories, with its focus on the relationship of forms to contents and functions, can still be a means to a better understanding of the nature and the power of stories.

Chapter 7

Conclusion and Recommendations

In this chapter, the conclusion for the present study and some recommendations for further research will be provided.

7.1. Structural Analysis of Burmese Folk Tales

As discussed in chapter 2, a number of studies have used different methods to explore the structures of narrative in general and folk tales in particular. This has led to various descriptions of different models. What is lacking in most of the models is an explanation of how the fundamental events interlock with one another to create a plot and how formal patterns are related to the story's content.

The present study has made an attempt not only to identify the functional events and possible structural patterns in Burmese folk tales but also to investigate the links between the functional events and between the episodic moves of a tale. By exploring the logical links based on the concept of sequential meaning, the study has dealt with the form as well as the content of a tale and also pre-empted the possible criticism that it has disregarded the content in the search for the form. Moreover, using two common structural patterns identified in the analysis of tales, the study has also shown some possibilities of discovering the relationship between the form or narrative structure of a tale and its function (social purpose) and field (narrative content). Through a comparison of the narrative structures in similar tales from different cultures, the study has proposed using a structural analysis of tales as a means to gain insights into the cultural determination of narrative content and the social purpose of storytelling.

The analysis conducted in this study has also proved that a morphological classification of Burmese folk tales is possible. It shows the possibility of using structure, in addition to the purpose and theme of a tale, as alternative criteria in categorising folk tales into different types. The study has shown, through an analysis of how the functional events are combined into a storyline, that tales can be compared from the standpoint of structure. With regard to the structural analysis of a story, Bal (1985) has cautioned, 'one should not refer to *the* structure of a fabula, but *a* structure' (p. 23; emphasis in original), for the events can be related in a variety of ways. Attempts to find out a single sequence will only lead to the rigid homogeneity of a plot, which is not typical of different tale types (Bal, 1985). Taking this caveat into consideration, the study has classified 27 Burmese folk tales from a collection into five different types, according to their similarities in the functional events and combination sequences. The classification made in this study is different from that made by the collector Maung Htin Aung, which is based on the thematic resemblance of the tales. Problems with thematic categorisations caused by the inconsistency in the choice of criterion have been pointed out by Abbott and Khin (2000). Varied classification of tales on the basis of their subject matter or themes has also been criticised by Martin (1986) as a violation of the basic principles of classification because they are not based on clear-cut conceptual distinctions.

The analysis in this study has also shown how the structural analysis of folk tales can be explored using an interdisciplinary approach. For an investigation of the linkage of events into overarching storylines, the study has adapted a narrative dimension of linearity, which is proposed by Ochs and Capps (2001) in their analysis of everyday storytelling or conversational narrative. By incorporating Propp's (1968) framework for identifying functional events in folk tales and Ochs and Capps' (2001) narrative dimension of linearity for an investigation of the linkage among these events, the study has shown how an analysis of functional events in folk tales can be complemented with the application of recent work in an allied discipline.

7.2. Recommendations

There are a number of areas that future research can examine for a study of folk tales or narrative or storytelling. What follows are some recommendations for those who would like to explore these areas further. It is hoped that a structural analysis of folk tales can become a means rather than an end, as has always been suggested by the scholars adopting a structural approach to narrative.

7.2.1. Oral Storytelling

The present study has focused only on the oral tales in their printed forms as they appear in a book. The functional events, the different models, and the linkage among those events in each model discovered in this study are expected to serve as a stable 'what' for the discussion on the 'how' of storytelling in future research. Linearity can still be a dimension to measure the narrative proclivities in various actual storytelling contexts, as it has been used by Ochs and Capps (2001) to explain the differences between telling a story *to* another and telling a story *with* another. That is to say, the texture and context of folk tales, in addition to the basic story structures, can be subjected to a structural analysis, as pointed out by Dundes (1971, 1980). From the aspect of texture, a comparative study can be done on the textural realisations of a tale recorded in two languages, for example. From the aspect of context, one can study the narrative structures of these tales in different actual storytelling contexts in which the teller may dramatise and the audience may interact, participate, or interrupt.

Various structural patterns found in this analysis of folk tales can help us to understand and discuss how a storyteller enables to repeat a tale, generate a new tale, revise a tale, complicate an old tale, or even make it possible to leave it up to the listeners how they want the tale to end. For example, in a study of Bulu (African) folk tales, Horner (1970) has implied that the structure of a tale can be open-ended and dependent on the choice of the listener when the tale ends, '…we ask you gentle reader (or listener) how you would settle this delicate question?' (Horner, 1970, p. 21). Similarly, it can be deduced from MacDonald's (1999b) examination of the functions of storytelling that the extent to which listeners are allowed to express and acknowledge emotions during an actual storytelling performance could vary from event to event or from culture to culture. The possibility of open-endedness in telling a story will explain, in part, how (in contrast to the basic story structure) the actual textual realisation of tales in one collection can differ widely or slightly from those collected by different collectors at different times or in different places.

How the story form is affected by the involvement of the audience, or with the change of the context in storytelling, can be studied as a move from a text-centred analysis towards a context-oriented analysis, as recommended by Rimmon-Kenan (2002). However, it is suggested here that a study of the complexity of the teller's interaction with the audience will require a different approach because other narrative dimensions, such as tellership, tellability, embeddedness, and moral stance (Ochs & Capps, 2001) will be brought into attention.

7.2.2. Multimodality and Oral Storytelling Performances

Closely related to the studies of folk tales in actual storytelling contexts, an analysis of the narrative structures in folk tales can also complement or be complemented by a performance-based multimodal analysis of actual oral storytelling processes. Such studies can be done to find out how a storyteller employs features from different modes (e.g., verbal, vocal, and visual) to achieve the aesthetic and communicative effectiveness during an actual storytelling process.

According to Kress and van Leeuwen (2001), multimodality is the use of several semiotic modes and their interactions within a sociocultural domain, which result in a semiotic product or event. In the case of an oral storytelling performance, apparently spoken words and the storyteller's voice (i.e., verbal and vocal features) are the primary means of communication. As Sawyer (1976) noted: 'our instrument is our voice; that we work with, and by means of, the spoken language—words' (p. 131). At the same time, the bodily presence of the storyteller allows them to use gestures, postures, and facial expressions, and thus brings in one more semiotic channel (i.e., the visual). Indeed, an oral storytelling performance can be regarded as a synaesthetic activity with the verbal, vocal, and visual aspects occurring at the same time (Miller, 1996). Each of these aspects represents a dimension of communication, and all these dimensions in combination lead to a characteristic called multidimensionality in oral storytelling (Lipman, 1999).

Most of the time, however, oral tales are analysed only after they have been transformed into printed texts. As a result, although it is apparent that oral storytelling is an infusion of features from verbal, vocal, and visual aspects, vocal and visual features (and some verbal features as well) are often left out in the studies of oral tales. With little reference made to the storyteller's actions and the actual storytelling process, the textual realisation of an oral tale is often examined as a finished product, like that of a written narrative, rather than as a process that involves more than one semiotic mode. Given that an oral story takes its negotiated and situation-specific shape only once during the process of telling (Livo & Reitz, 1986), verbal as well as nonverbal features employed by the storyteller during a storytelling process should all be regarded as parts of the anatomy of an oral tale. Accordingly, the textual realisation of an oral tale can be appropriately examined as dynamics unfolded during the storytelling process.

Various features employed by a storyteller during a storytelling process can be analysed according to the three major aspects of expression: verbal, vocal, and visual. Verbal features refer to those related to the use of a specific form of language, such as discourse markers, expressive elaboration, direct address to the audience, quotation from dialogues/monologues, syntactic parallelism, and so on. Conversely, vocal features denote manipulations of voice by a storyteller during a storytelling process. Features such as pitch, pace, volume, pause, inflection, and tone can be examined. As regards features from the visual aspect, the most fundamental features, which are inseparably linked to the presence of the storyteller in this type of storytelling—their spontaneous and synchronised gestures (and facial expressions)—should also be studied.

Given that expressive features from verbal, vocal, and visual aspects can be employed more or less simultaneously at any one point of a storytelling process, an analysis of features working at each dimension should be followed by an examination of how features from different dimensions interact with one another to represent elements of the story and to encourage desired responses from the audience. To capture the different sign systems that work together during the storytelling process, live performances of folk tales need to be audio and video recorded. The data then need to be presented as 'a performable script' (Tedlock, 1983), in other words, transcriptions of the storytelling discourse that include notations of verbal, vocal, and visual features employed by the storyteller. Features from each semiotic channel can then be noted in succinct word descriptions in separate columns. For a multimodal analysis of a storytelling performance, it is important to capture the different sign systems that work together during the storytelling process.

It would also be interesting to find out how features from verbal, vocal, and visual aspects work in concert to create various narrative effects that promote emotive responses from the audience. For example, as the storyline approaches the climax, increasingly detailed verbal representation of the character's actions may synchronise with an increasingly faster pace and louder volume. When this is visually complemented by a combination of gestures representing moment-by-moment actions of the character, the result can be an effect that promotes a sense of urgency and excitement for the audience.

Such studies may discover unexpected patterns in the way storytellers employ resources from different channels to achieve the aesthetic and communicative effectiveness throughout the storytelling process. In this way, such studies can help us understand how storytelling has expanded its role as a traditional form of entertainment to a powerful communicative tool in many institutions in contemporary society—schools, libraries, and museums—as noted by folklore scholars and storytellers such as MacDonald (1999a) and Sobol (2008).

Telling stories face-to-face with an audience as a live performance is often associated with folk tales, and it is often regarded as one of the oldest forms of oral art. In contemporary society, this kind of storytelling is receiving a renewed interest from various institutions as an effective means to cultivate institutional values and disseminate institutional messages. Folk tales from various cultures are often used by professional storytellers as a way of communicating institutional messages during specially scheduled sessions in places like schools, libraries, and museums, especially for children. The emergence of new forms of live oral storytelling has led folklorists and anthropologists, with their interest in oral literature or oral traditions of a society, to delimit the folkloristic type of storytelling only to those performances in which storytellers learn their stories solely through oral sources (Pellowski, 1990). In practice, such folkloristic storytelling is preserved only in certain cultures and societies in the modern age. What is more commonly found to exist today as traditional face-to-face storytelling is live storytelling performances in various institutions.

Like folkloristic storytelling, institutionalised live oral storytelling also carries such characteristics as performative and communal quality, simple narrative structures with similar repetitive forms, and some counterintuitive elements in narrative contents. However, unlike folkloristic storytelling, the settings and subject matter of institutionalised storytelling are determined by the institutional purposes of storytelling, rather than the culture. Thus, studies of this type of storytelling should examine how the cultural content of folk tales are adapted by revivalist storytellers to suit and appeal to the tastes of today's audiences, which in most cases are likely to be multicultural and multiracial.

7.2.3. Comparative Studies of Narrative Structures

More work can also be done by those who are interested in narrative structures of folk tales in their written form. Exploration of the narrative structures in folk tales, as a simple form of narrative, has resulted in descriptions of different models. However, as pointed out by Jason and Segal (1977), 'the development in the structural analysis of oral literature has not been cumulative' because each investigator 'goes his own way and explores his own path of inquiry' (p. 7). Most of the studies on narrative structures are conducted on a collection of tales from a particular culture or a particular type of tale. For example, Zipes (2000) noted that the fairy tale, upon which Propp's study was completed, is only one type of literary appropriation of a particular oral storytelling tradition related to oral wonder tales. Moreover, some of the assumptions and theoretical frameworks, which have been introduced under the influence of formalism and structuralism, came under attack in the poststructuralist period (Rimmon-Kenan, 2002).

Thus, an area that warrants further research is the comparative studies of the narrative structures in folk tales of adjacent countries that are likely to have some influence on each other's culture. In most (if not all) cases, the influence of cultures from neighbouring countries results in sharing many common cultural features. Therefore, it would be interesting to examine:

1. How far is Propp correct in postulating that the sequence of functions is basically always the same? How feasible is it to postulate potential sequences of functions in folk tales of adjacent countries with similar cultures?
2. What are the fundamental elements constituting the prevalent structural patterns in folk tales of Southeast Asian countries, and how are they linked into coherent and well-organised storylines?
3. What elements can be claimed as transcultural and what are culture-specific in relation to aspects of the narrative of Southeast Asian folk tales?
4. Do any systematic recurrent patterns in Southeast Asian folk tales conform to patterns common elsewhere, and does such conformity lead to any possibility of proposing some models as the structural potential of this narrative genre?

In addition to the analysis of narrative structures in the folk tales of each culture per se, a comparative study on tales of various types from some adjacent countries in Southeast Asia, each with a similar but unique culture, is expected to give some plausible answers to these questions. There have been some publications on the collection of folk tales from Southeast Asian nations. Some of these include:

ASEAN Folk Literature: An Anthology (Eugenio, 1995)
Cambodian Folk Stories From the Gatiloke (Carrison, 1987)
Indonesian Folktales (Bunanta, 2003)

Lao Folktales (Tossa, 2008)
Thai Folk Tales (Jumsai & Luang, 1977)
The Singing Top: Tales From Malaysia, Singapore, and Brunei (MacDonald, 2008)

With the selection of the most representative, and in some cases the most popular, examples of the most important types of folk literature in each country, these valuable collections have revealed what the folk literatures of some Southeast Asian countries have in common and what is unique to each country. The collection of folk tales in these publications, as a type of folk narrative in prose, has also shown some interesting similarities, in terms of the narrative motif or the content. It is also noted that there are 'local versions of well-known international folktale types' (Eugenio, 1995, p. 10). However, the classifications of tales in most of these collections are based on their thematic similarities, which have been commented on by some scholars (e.g., Abbott & Khin, 2001; Martin, 1986) for the inconsistency in the choice of criteria and for not being based on clear-cut conceptual distinctions in a few cases.

Thus, a study can be proposed to investigate the structural similarities and differences in the folk tales of Southeast Asian nations. Such studies will enable us to make a cross-cultural morphological classification by comparing them from the standpoint of the story structure. While any distinctiveness in the storylines of the folk tales from a Southeast Asian nation will highlight its uniqueness in respect to the narrative structures of a particular culture, the structural likeness across tales of different cultures can lead to some typical storylines, which can be claimed to be translinguistic and transcultural. Systematic recurrent patterns in Southeast Asian folk tales may also conform to patterns common elsewhere. This potential analogy of folk-tale structures may add on the possibility of finding some structural potential capable of denoting certain narratives as belonging to the folk-tale genre and also of generating narratives in this genre.

These studies can also search for other elements, such as narrative roles, episodes, and causality, which can be claimed as necessary for a coherent and well-organised plot structure in folk tales. Such elements can be compared across tales from different cultures, so that the affinities as well as the uniqueness in relation to aspects of the narrative of Southeast Asian folk tales can be fully discovered. With the findings on the universal or culture-specific narrative structures in Southeast Asian folk tales, these studies can then examine the possibility of proposing some models that can be viewed in terms of the structural potential of the folk-tale genre. With the advancement of technology and increasing interest in digital storytelling, findings from these studies about the structural potential of the folk-tale genre can give some hopes for the development of a computer programme capable of generating tales that possibly combine elements from more than one culture.

7.2.4. Tale Generators and Narrativity

According to Propp, a uniform plot progression can be formed by connecting a series of any set of the 31 functions in order. This assertion has become a subject of dispute. Commenting on the results of an experiment by Klein and colleagues at generating sample texts of 'folk tales' with the help of a computer programme, Jason and Segal (1977) suggested:

> It is also necessary to take into account the constraints imposed on the cooccurrence [*sic*] of elements along the syntagmatic axis. There is hope that if and when this additional semantic analysis is added to Propp's scheme, the computer will produce much more verisimilar texts. (p. 6)

Similarly, through an exploration of Proppian structural analysis, Lim, Tan, and Wee (2001) have experimented with a contemporary rewriting of tales, using a computing programme. In their experiment on the electronic 'Proppian Fairy Tale Generator', the results are usually an oddly coherent narrative, flitting in and out of focus, when the generator works by randomly choosing a possible interpretation of a function from Propp's 31 functions, and stringing them together to create a story.

These studies demonstrate that it is necessary to consider several other elements, besides functions, in order to create a coherent and well-written tale. The formalist and descriptive frameworks in the study of story structures need to be reconsidered and advanced into interpretative and evaluative models, with the application of recent findings in related disciplines. Although it has generally been believed that the proclivity towards constructing an overarching storyline that ties events together in a seamless explanatory framework has been the focus of folklore (Ochs & Capps, 2001), it still remains to be proved how the structures of folk tales contribute to this proclivity and achieve narrativity in an identical or in various ways.

Narrativity designates not only 'the set of properties characterising narratives and distinguishing them from non-narratives', but also 'the set of optional features that make narratives more prototypically narrative-like, more immediately identified, processed, and interpreted as narratives' (Prince, 2005, p. 387). It is not surprising that narrativity particularly poses problems for those who are interested in programming a tale generator. Within the framework of narratology (i.e., the theory and the study of narrative and its structures), narrative theorists have made attempts to determine what makes a text narrative, through an examination of the formal characteristics claimed to be common to all and only narratives. A sequence of causally related events is often regarded as the most fundamental characteristic of a narrative in traditional narratological investigations. In other words, with the focus on the identification of the components and their order within a text that make it a narrative, these studies have defined narrativeness as a generic term, referring to all narratives. Conversely, narrativity is related to the factors reflecting an interpretative framework that storytellers and recipients might use to judge a text as more or less narrative. Thus, narrativity has more of its focus on the single narrative, and different narrative texts can be proved to constitute different kinds or different degrees of narrativity.

Studies of narrativity have focused on the plot structures or the recipient's cognitive processes or the combination of plot structures and cognitive processes. For example, Prince (1997) focused on the plot structures and outlined the elements that, according to him, are conducive to and thus able to affect the degree of narrativity in a text. According to Prince (1997), the narrativity of a text 'depends on the extent to which the text is taken to constitute a (pointed) autonomous whole' (p. 42) that

(a) represents an anthropomorphic project;
(b) involves some kind of conflict;
(c) is made up of discrete, particular, positive, and temporally distinct actions that have logically unpredictable antecedents or consequences; and
(d) avoids inordinate amounts of commentary about them, their representation, or the latter's context.

It is also contended that 'all other things being equal, the presence of disnarrated elements (representing what did not happen but could have) affected narrativity in a positive manner' (Prince, 2001, p. 29). Such a plot-based definition of narrativity does not explain the pragmatic factors, for example how receivers react to the structural components of a text in specifying narrativity.

Conversely, from the perspective of cognitive science, Polkinghorne contended that 'storytelling and story comprehension are ultimately grounded in the general human capacity to conceptualize—that is, to structure experiential elements into wholes' (1991, p. 142). Following such claims, human consciousness or experientiality can be regarded as playing a crucial role in specifying narrativity. This notion of experientiality has been developed into a proposal to redefine narrativity in terms of cognitive parameters by Fludernik (1996, 2003). Fludernik equated narrativity with experientiality, and argued that '*narrativity is a function of narrative texts and centres on experientiality of an anthropomorphic nature*' (Fludernik, 1996, p. 26, emphasis in original). She disqualified the criteria of sequentiality and logical connectedness in a plot from playing the central role in defining narrativity (Fludernik, 1996, 2003). Instead, she has shifted the emphasis to the receptional and creative aspect. She focused on the consciousness or experientiality of an actant, which she regarded as an *existent* that is prototypically human. Fludernik claimed that experientiality combines a number of cognitively relevant factors, such as 'the presence of a human protagonist', 'her experience of events as they impinge on her situation or activity', and 'the protagonist's emotional and physical reaction to this constellation' (Fludernik, 1996, p. 30). Narrativity is said to emerge from such 'experiential portrayal of dynamic event sequences which are already configured emotively and evaluatively' or to 'consist in the experiential depiction of human consciousness *tout court*' (Fludernik, 1996, p. 30).

Fludernik's proposal to equate narrativity with experientiality in every narrative genre has become a subject of dispute. For example, Alber (2002) has pointed out some problems caused by Fludernik's rejection of all plot-oriented definitions of narrativity. These problems include what in a text can account for the projection of experientiality that makes it narrative and not something else, and how one can specify different degrees of narrativity on the basis of experientiality. According to Alber, Fludernik's 'experientiality first, plot later' approach could make almost every text a narrative. Therefore, Alber (2002) insisted that

> for such a distinction, categories like plot, action, character, 'real-world' setting, all of which Fludernik attempts to play down in her paradigm, turn out to be crucial after all. (p. 69)

Thus, subsequent studies of narrativity (e.g., Herman, 2002; Ryan, 1992) have recognised the inadequacies to specify narrativity exclusively on the basis of a text's plot structures or exclusively from the aspect of recipients' cognitive responses. Scholars have tried to include both components—a text's plot structures as well as recipients' cognitive processes—in their explorations of narrativity. For example, Ryan (1992) proposed a model in which she examined 'the role of narrative structures in the textual economy', and 'the mental operations necessary to retrieve and/or to properly evaluate the narrative structure' (pp. 369–384). In other words, Ryan's specification of narrativity is based on the analysis of narrative structures in a given text and the interpretation of these structures in the process of comprehending it. The semantic domain projected by a given text is regarded as a textual economy, and the role of the story is assessed with respect to the whole of the text, taking both narrative and nonnarrative elements into consideration.

These studies suggest that in addition to the structural potential of the folk-tale genre, which promises a possibility of developing a fairy tale or folk tale generator, resources from language theory and cognitive science are needed for an understanding of how folk tales have the proclivity towards constructing an overarching storyline that ties events together in a seamless explanatory framework and that also meets the receiver's desire for a complete whole.

7.2.5. From Folk Tales to Other Genres of Folklore

Dundes, in his introduction to Propp's (1968) *Morphology of the Folktale*, suggested applying Propp's framework to genres of folklore other than folk tales, such as proverbs and tongue-twisters. The discovery of the structures in fairy tales can also lead to such questions as 'Do the children become familiar enough with the general nature of fairy tale morphology to object or question a deviation from it by a storyteller?' The findings of narrative structures in folk tales can be put to the service of cultural and ideological concerns as well as to the study of nonnarrative and nonverbal semiotic objects.

Appendix A

Titles of the Tales in the Collection

Folk Tales of Burma by Maung Htin Aung (1976)

Tale 1 'The Cat Who Pretended to Be a University Professor'
Tale 2 'The Lapwing and the Lay Brother'
Tale 3 'Why the Snail's Muscles Never Ache?'
Tale 4 'The Four Drums of Destiny'
Tale 5 'Mister Luck and Mister Industry'
Tale 6 'How Master Thumb Defeated the Sun?'
Tale 7 'The Golden Crow'
Tale 8 'The Drunkard and the Opium Eater'
Tale 9 'The Big Tortoise'
Tale 10 'Jealous of Others, Suffer Own Loss'
Tale 11 'Not Angry, but Buffalo Tails Have Become Short'
Tale 12 'How the Opium Eater Went to Heaven?'
Tale 13 'The Great King Eats Chaff'
Tale 14 'The Four Deaf Men'
Tale 15 'The Drunkard and the Threatening Ghost'
Tale 16 'The Poor Scholar and the Alchemist'
Tale 17 'The Greedy Stall-Keeper and the Poor Traveller'
Tale 18 'Why Female Elephants Hate Pregnant Women'
Tale 19 'The Sun, the Moon, and the Evening Star'
Tale 20 'When the Gods Played Hide and Seek'
Tale 21 'The Origin of Fire'

Tale 22 'The Egg Born King'
Tale 23 'The Magic Cock'
Tale 24 'The Hundred and One Lobsters'
Tale 25 'The Snail Prince'
Tale 26 'Khun San Law and Nan Oo Pyin'
Tale 27 'The Origin of the Rainy Season'

Appendix B

Female Fairy Tale

Tale 9: 'The Big Tortoise'
Distribution of characters in narrative roles:
Villain: Stepmother
Protagonist A (Heroine): Mistress Youngest
Protagonist B (False Heroine): Stepsister
Helper: The Mother (transfigured into a Tortoise and a Gold and Silver tree), the Neighbours, the Servant, the Old Man, and His Wife

'The Big Tortoise'[9]	Events
Once there lived a fisherman and his wife, and they had a very beautiful daughter by the name of Mistress Youngest. The mother was very fond of the daughter, but the father was a little indifferent. One day, the couple went out fishing in a boat, and for some hours the husband could not catch anything at all. He became very short-tempered, whereas his wife became anxious lest she should not be able to cook any fish for her daughter. After great trouble a fish was caught, and the wife cried, 'This is for Mistress Youngest and not for sale'. Another was caught, and the wife again cried out, 'I claim this for Mistress Youngest'. The husband became very angry at this	Move 1 Information connective—Protagonist A is introduced.
and hit her with an oar, and she fell into the sea and was transformed into a big tortoise. The fisherman, of	Event 1. Absence

(*continued on next page*)

(*continued*)

'The Big Tortoise'[9]	Events
course, thought that she was drowned. When he arrived back at his village, he simply said that his wife fell into the sea and was drowned. Everybody assumed that it was all an unfortunate accident, and everyone felt sorry for the fisherman over his loss.	
After some time, the fisherman decided to marry again, and he chose as his spouse a hateful old witch. She was a widow and had a daughter by her first marriage. The daughter was a sour-tempered young woman with an ugly face made uglier by pockmarks. Both the mother and the daughter were jealous of Mistress Youngest because she was so beautiful and kind, and between them they made her life a misery. They made her do all the housework, and they scolded her and jeered at her. The fisherman took no interest in Mistress Youngest and just left her to the tender mercies of his wife and stepdaughter.	Information connective—Villain and Protagonist B (False Heroine) are introduced. Event 8a. Lack
One afternoon, Mistress Youngest felt so unhappy that she slipped out of her house and went to the seashore. There she sat down and cried her heart out. Presently, she saw an old tortoise swimming towards her and, to her surprise, she saw that the old tortoise was crying also. Now she guessed that the old tortoise was her mother, and she took the animal in her arms. The tortoise, of course, could not speak to her, but it seemed so pleased to be with Mistress Youngest. So every afternoon Mistress Youngest came to the seashore and stayed with the tortoise until nightfall.	Event 11. Departure Event 15. Guidance Event 19. Liquidation
After a few days, the stepmother and the stepsister noticed that, in spite of their ill treatment, Mistress Youngest seemed happier than before, and also that she disappeared from the house every afternoon. So they followed her to the seashore and saw her sitting and talking to the tortoise. They were very furious that Mistress Youngest should have any friends, and they decided to deprive Mistress Youngest of her happy afternoons.	Move 2 Transfer connective. Event 4. Reconnaissance Event 5. Delivery

(*continued on next page*)

(continued)

'The Big Tortoise'[9]	Events
The next morning, the stepmother made a lot of crisp and dry pancakes, and put them under her bed. When her husband returned from his work in the afternoon, the stepmother, pretending to be very ill, lay in bed; when she turned this way and that way, naturally the cakes underneath her made a crackling noise and she moaned repeatedly: 'This side I turn, crackle, crackle, That side I turn, crackle, crackle, I die of splintered bones'.	Event 6. Trickery
The husband became so anxious that he rushed out and brought back the village physician. The physician had been bribed beforehand by the stepmother, so he looked at the patient and said that it was a serious disease, but the remedy was easy. 'Give her tortoise flesh at once', he prescribed, 'and she will be all right in no time'.	Event 7. Complicity
'How fortunate!' exclaimed the patient. 'My daughter tells me that a big, fat tortoise comes to the shore every afternoon, and so my husband can easily go and catch it at once'. Then the stepmother led the fisherman to the place where Mistress Youngest was sitting with the tortoise in her arms. The fisherman, in spite of the tearful entreaties for the animal's life on the part of Mistress Youngest, killed the tortoise at once, and ordered Mistress Youngest to cook it quickly for her stepmother.	Event 8. Villainy
Poor Mistress Youngest! How she cried and cried in the kitchen as she prepared her stepmother's dinner. She was stricken with grief and the work was tiring. As the tortoise was an exceptionally big one, she had to wash more than a hundred dishes to contain all the cooked flesh. At last all was ready, and the stepmother jumped up from bed, saying that the mere smell of the tortoise flesh had cured her. She invited her husband and daughter to share the meal with her. Out of sheer malice, she also invited Mistress Youngest who, of course, declined, saying that she was unwell. As there	Event 8a. Lack

(continued on next page)

(*continued*)

'The Big Tortoise'[9]	Events
were so many dishes of tortoise flesh, the stepmother decided to send one dish to each neighbour, because her treatment of the gentle Mistress Youngest had made her unpopular with the neighbours and she wanted to become popular. So she ordered Mistress Youngest to take a dish to every cottage in the village with her compliments.	
At every cottage Mistress Youngest was asked, 'What could we do to make you happy?' and she always replied, 'Please eat the flesh, but do not throw away the bones. Please keep the bones in the eaves of your cottage, so that I can come and collect them without disturbing you'. Late that night, she went from cottage to cottage and brought back the bones from the eaves. Then she buried the bones just outside her cottage door, and she made this oath: 'If I truly love my mother, may a tree of gold and silver fruit grow here to mark her grave'. Early the next day, all the neighbours	Event 15. Guidance
were surprised to see a wonderful tree which seemed to have grown overnight, right in front of the cottage of the fisherman. It was indeed a wonderful tree, for some of its fruit were of silver, and others were of gold. As the neighbours stood around and gaped at the tree, the king of the country passed by on his hunting elephant. 'A gold and silver tree in this remote village!' he said, 'and who owns it?'	Event 15. Guidance
The stepmother came out of the cottage and answered, 'My daughter owns it, Your Majesty'.	
'Call her then', ordered the king, and the stepsister came forward. 'Is that your tree?' asked the king.	
'Yes. Your Majesty', answered the stepsister.	
'If that is so, pluck your fruit and come with me', ordered the king. The stepsister climbed up the tree and, although she pulled with all her strength, the fruit could not be plucked. 'I don't believe you own the tree', said the king with a frown, 'and I wonder who is the real owner'.	

(*continued on next page*)

(*continued*)

'The Big Tortoise'[9]	Events
'We think Mistress Youngest owns it, Your Majesty', said the neighbours. The king summoned Mistress Youngest to his presence and asked her to prove that the tree belonged to her. So Mistress Youngest sat under the tree and made this oath: 'If this tree belongs to me, may all the fruits fall into my lap', and all the fruits fell into her lap. The king was very pleased, and took her away on his elephant to the capital where she was crowned as queen. The stepmother and stepsister gnashed their teeth in anger and malice, and they cut down the tree out of sheer spite.	Event 19. Liquidation
After four or five months, the stepmother and the stepsister thought of a plan to kill Mistress Youngest, and so they sent word to her begging her to forgive them their past misdeeds and to come and stay with them for a few weeks. Mistress Youngest was a very kind and trusting young woman, and she believed them. So, asking permission from her husband, the king, she went to the village, taking only a few retainers, and these few she sent back the moment she reached her father's cottage, as she did not want her old friends in the village to think that she had become conceited with so many servants and followers round her. Before the retainers went away, however, she instructed them to come back after one month.	Move 3 Transfer connective. Event 6. Trickery Event 7. Complicity
The stepmother and the stepsister were outwardly very sweet and loving to Mistress Youngest, but all the time they were waiting eagerly for an opportunity to kill her. One day, while sitting at dinner, the stepmother dropped a spoon down a hole in the kitchen flooring, and Mistress Youngest, ever dutiful, thinking that the spoon had been dropped accidentally, went down to fetch it. When she was right underneath, the stepmother emptied a cauldron of boiling water over her, and poor Mistress Youngest was transformed into a white paddy-bird, which flew away swiftly.	Event 6. Trickery Event 7. Complicity Event 8. Villainy

(*continued on next page*)

(continued)

'The Big Tortoise'[9]	Events
On the appointed day, the retainers came back and they were met by the wicked stepsister who was dressed up in the fine raiment of Mistress Youngest. 'You are not our Queen', they exclaimed indignantly.	Move 4 Transfer connective.
'I am', replied the stepsister, 'but you cannot recognize me as I was attacked by the terrible disease of smallpox during your absence, and as a result my face is now disfigured'. The retainers were rather dubious, but all the same they had to escort her back to the king. When she arrived at the palace, the king said in anger, 'You are not Mistress Youngest, for your face is pockmarked, whereas her face was as fair as the lily'.	Event 24. Unfounded claims
'My lord', replied the stepsister, 'I was attacked by the terrible disease of smallpox. Will you discard me just because I contracted the disease through no fault of my own?'	
'You cannot be Mistress Youngest', said the king, 'For your forehead is high and ugly, unlike her beautiful forehead'.	
'I missed you so much, my Lord', replied the stepsister, 'that I often cried hitting my forehead against the floor, and it has now become swollen'.	Event 24. Unfounded claims
'You cannot be Mistress Youngest', said the king, 'For your nose is too long and ugly, so different from her beautiful nose'.	
'My Lord', replied the stepsister, 'I missed you so much that I was always weeping, and I had to wipe my nose so many times. No wonder my nose has become long'. The king, however, remained suspicious.	
Now Mistress Youngest was a wonderful weaver, and all the king's dresses were woven by her. Wanting to test the stepsister, he now asked her to weave a dress for him. The stepsister went to the weaving room, but as she was a fool with her hands she sat at the loom in great fear lest her lack of skill in weaving should	

(continued on next page)

(*continued*)

'The Big Tortoise'[9]	Events
show that she was an imposter. But Mistress Youngest, in the form of the paddy-bird, came to her rescue; for even as a bird, Mistress Youngest cared only for the happiness of her husband and wanted him to wear a fine dress. So the white paddy-bird flew into the weaving room by the window and, seizing the spindle in her beak, she wove a dress of a wonderful pattern. The stepsister watched the paddy-bird in silence until it had finished weaving and had dropped the spindle; then she picked up the spindle, and threw it at the paddy-bird, who fell down dead. She picked up the dead bird and, calling the cook, ordered him to roast it. When the king came into the room in the evening, she showed him the dress, and said, 'My Lord, the dress would have been even better had not a white paddy-bird come and interfered with my weaving'. The king had to admit that the dress was well woven but he remained wrapped in gloom, for he still suspected that the stepsister was an impostor.	Event 8. Villainy
The king sat down to dinner and a servant brought in the roasted paddy-bird. 'What is this?' asked the king.	
'It is that interfering paddy-bird', said the stepsister. 'I killed it and had it roasted specially for you'.	
'Poor little bird! I don't want to eat you', said the king, ordering his servant to take it away. The servant also felt sorry for the bird and, instead of eating it or throwing it away, he buried it behind the kitchen. The next day a big quince tree was seen growing behind the kitchen and the stepsister, being suspicious of trees which grow overnight, made careful inquiries, but nobody could say how the tree came to be there. The servant of the previous night, however, guessed that the tree had something to do with the paddy-bird, for the tree was growing out of the vary place where he had buried the bird; but he did not say anything as he was frightened of the stepsister.	Event 22. Rescue <u>Move 5</u> Transfer connective.

(*continued on next page*)

(continued)

'The Big Tortoise'[9]	Events
An old man and his wife came to the palace kitchen to sell their firewood. After selling it, they rested under the big quince tree and a big quince fruit fell on the woman's lap. 'Lucky it did not fall on our heads!' they laughed. They picked up the fruit meaning to eat it in the evening, but when they reached their home the woman thought that it was not ripe enough yet to be eaten. So she put it away in an earthen jar meaning to eat it a few days later. Early next morning, the couple went out as usual to gather firewood, and as usual they returned at breakfast time. They were astonished to find that in their absence the cottage had been swept clean, and the meal cooked. They looked everywhere, but could not find any trace of the stranger who had so kindly tidied up the cottage and cooked the meal. The next morning the same thing happened. 'I will solve the mystery tomorrow', whispered the old man to his wife that night, 'For I have thought of a plan'. Long before the first streak of daylight appeared the old man got up from the bed and, giving a nudge with his elbow to his wife, he cried loudly, 'You old lazybones, get up, get up, and let us go earlier than usual, so that we can gather more firewood'. The old woman, realizing that her husband wanted all the world to think that they were going out, said loudly in reply, 'You are the lazybones, for I am ready to go out now'. They went out of their cottage shouting and pretending to quarrel but, after they had gone half a mile, they came back stealthily in the darkness and, entering their cottage silently, they hid behind the door to watch. When the sun had risen, they saw a tiny little woman come out of the earthen jar and run into the kitchen. 'It is a fruit maiden', whispered the old woman, 'and I know how to catch her'. So saying she fetched one of her skirts and, spreading it, she stood by the jar. Then she gave a shout, which frightened the little fruit maiden, who now came running towards	Event 15. Guidance

(continued on next page)

(*continued*)

'The Big Tortoise'[9]	Events
the jar. The old woman threw the skirt over the fruit maiden, and Lo! Mistress Youngest stood before them. 'You are our queen', they said, recognizing her, 'and we must take you to our lord the king'. At first, Mistress Youngest refused as she did not want her stepsister to get into trouble, but in the end she agreed as she wanted to see her husband again so badly.	Event 17. Branding
The king and the stepsister were giving an audience to the courtiers when the old couple entered with Mistress Youngest. The king was very pleased to see Mistress Youngest again, but he was not too surprised at her return, for he had always suspected that the stepsister was an impostor.	Move 6 Transfer connective.
'But I am Mistress Youngest', protested the stepsister, 'and this woman is an impostor and a witch. She has bewitched you all to make you think that she is I'.	Event 24. Unfounded claims
'She is the true Mistress Youngest', said the old couple, who then proceeded to relate how they had found Mistress Youngest.	Event 23. Unrecognised arrival
'Didn't I tell you?' shouted the stepsister in triumph. 'A fruit maiden, and a witch I should say!' Mistress Youngest then told the king how she was first transformed into a paddy-bird, and then into a fruit maiden.	
'I demand that the custom of the people should be followed in this case', exclaimed the stepsister, 'and I demand a trial by ordeal'. Now in a trial by ordeal, the parties to dispute had to fight a duel with swords; but, whereas the defendant was allowed to fight with an iron sword, the plaintiff had to use a wooden one, for on the plaintiff was the burden of proof and it was assumed that, if justice was really on his side, he would win in spite of the fact that his sword was wooden. But the stepsister had no faith in a trial by ordeal; she thought that she would be able to kill Mistress Youngest with one stroke of her iron sword.	Event 25. Difficult task

(*continued on next page*)

(*continued*)

'The Big Tortoise'[9]	Events
The king and his courtiers were certain that the stepsister was an impostor and did not want to put Mistress Youngest to the ordeal; but what could they do? For even the king was not above the customary law of the people, and the stepsister's demand was a legitimate one. The king now ordered that the two swords be brought, and the wooden one given to Mistress Youngest, for she was the plaintiff and it was for her to prove her case. Mistress Youngest faced her stepsister, and made this oath: 'If I am really Mistress Youngest, may my stepsister's sword become harmless to me'. So, she stood there calmly, making no attempt to use her wooden sword, while the stepsister hewed and hacked at her with the iron sword. But Mistress Youngest remained unscathed, for the iron sword became as soft as velvet whenever it touched her body. Suddenly, the wooden sword, of its own accord, slipped out of Mistress Youngest's hand and cut off the stepsister's head.	Event 26. Solution Event 27. Recognition
The king decided that the stepmother should be made to suffer as well, although Mistress Youngest pleaded for her pardon. Accordingly, he gave orders that the dead body of the stepsister be first cut into pieces, and then put into a jar and pickled. Afterwards, he sent the jar to the stepmother with the message that it was a special gift of pickled fish made by the queen herself. The old stepmother was so proud of the royal gift that she asked her husband to come and taste the pickle at once. As she served out spoonful after spoonful, she kept chattering about her dear daughter, the queen, until the husband lost his temper and said, 'Woman, don't talk rubbish, but eat on'.	Event 28. Exposure Event 30. Punishment
The stepmother took out another spoonful from the jar, and cried out in alarm, 'This looks like a human finger, my daughter's finger'.	
'Don't talk rubbish', said the irate husband, 'but eat on'.	

(*continued on next page*)

(continued)

'The Big Tortoise'[9]	Events
She took out another spoonful and cried out in alarm, 'This looks like a human toe, my daughter's toe'.	
'Don't talk rubbish', said the irate husband, 'but eat on'.	
The stepmother peeped into the jar to see whether there was any pickle left, and she saw at the bottom the pockmarked face of her daughter, 'It is my daughter, it is my daughter', she wailed. At this the husband got up and beat her soundly for talking nonsense.	Event 30. Punishment

Appendix C

Summaries of Tales 22, 24, 25, 26, and 27

Tale 22: 'The Egg-Born King'

A young Shan herdsman and a dragon princess fell in love with each other. The dragon princess laid an egg and gave it to the herdsman before disappearing into the waters. A human son was born from the egg, and the son went to see his mother when he turned sixteen. The mother, the dragon princess, promised to help her son should harm befall on him. The king of a neighbouring nation had a beautiful daughter. The king put her in a golden tower on an island in the middle of a stormy lake. The king announced that whoever could reach the tower without using a log or a raft or a boat would marry his daughter. Hundreds of young men tried and drowned. The egg-born young man asked his mother, the dragon princess, for help. The mother helped him to reach the tower. The young man married the king's daughter and became the king of the neighbouring nation after some years. Four sons were born to them but they could not succeed the king because the throne must be returned to the people of the neighbouring nation. The king made each son become the king of one of his own four Shan kingdoms.

Tale 24: 'The Hundred and One Lobsters'

There was once a king who had a sow, a cow, a buffalo, and an elephant as his pets. One day, an old fisherman gave the king a hundred and one magical lobsters and said that any young woman who could eat them at one sitting would give birth to wonderful children. A young woman succeeded in eating all the lobsters and was made a junior queen. She gave birth to one hundred sons and one daughter. The chief queen was jealous of the junior queen and replaced the children with pups. The king was ashamed when he heard that the junior queen gave birth to pups, so he made her a lowly attendant. The one hundred and one children thrown away by the chief queen were saved by the king's pets, (the sow, then the cow, then the buffalo, and the elephant) before each of these pets was killed due to the chief queen's wicked trickery. The children were finally saved by a hermit and became the foster sons and daughter of a fisherman and his wife. After some time, the king held a cock fight and the children went to the palace to pitch their cock against the king's. The children met their mother and challenged the king that if their cock won, their mother be given to them. The children won the fight and their mother was given to them. The chief queen's villainy was exposed and she was punished. The children's mother was made the chief queen.

Tale 25: 'The Snail Prince'

Once the queen gave birth to a snail with a shell on its back. The king felt ashamed and ordered that the queen be made a gardener and the snail be floated down the river. The snail was picked up by the queen of the ogres. The snail changed into a little boy. The ogress took care of him. When the young man turned sixteen, he asked permission to travel up the river and live among human beings. The ogress gave him a magic cane and a magic cloak that turned him into an ugly little hunchback. The young man reached a city and worked as a cowherd. In that city, the king's youngest daughter was planning to select a husband by throwing her garland of jasmine flowers into the air. The garland fell on the head of the hunchback, so the hunchback married the princess and moved into the palace. After some time, the king prepared to choose a successor among his sons-in-law. He set a task and only the hunchback, among all his sons-in-law, was able to accomplish it with the help of the magic cane. The hunchback threw off his magic cloak and turned into a handsome golden prince. The snail prince was declared by his father-in-law to be the new king. The snail prince went to the city of his own father and demanded that his mother be restored to her old glory as the queen.

Tale 26: 'Khun San Law and Nan Oo Pyin'

Khun San Law's mother died when he was six, and he was adopted by a rich widow. The widow persuaded him to marry an ugly girl who had fallen in love with him. Khun San Law was not pleased with her, so he asked for his mother's permission to go away with the merchants who were leaving the village. Khun San Law met a beautiful girl, Nan Oo Pyin, at a market town. They fell in love and got married. After a few weeks he decided to go home to inform his mother of the marriage. He promised his wife to return in a few weeks. The mother, although she was furious and disapproving of the marriage, pretended to be pleased. She sent him to a faraway place as a way of parting him from his wife. Nan Oo Pyin, when her husband did not return as promised, travelled to Khun San Law's village. Khun San Law's mother, the old widow, overworked, abused, beat, and humiliated her. She returned to her own village, feeling sick and dying. The angry neighbours told Khun San Law about his mother's cruel treatment to his wife when he returned from the faraway place. He followed her, but she was already dead when he arrived. He died soon after. The bodies of the two lovers were laid side by side. The old widow, feeling jealous and angry when she saw the two bodies side by side, placed a bamboo carrying pole with three joints between them. Khun San Law and Nan Oo Pyin became twin stars in the sky, but between them was the bamboo carrying-pole with three joints appearing as the three other stars separating them.

Tale 27: 'The Origin of the Rainy Season'

The mother of a beautiful, good-natured girl died, and her father married again. The stepmother was unkind and jealous of the little girl. The girl was unhappy and lonely until she became friends with two little fish in the river. The stepmother learned about the two little fish and killed them using wicked trickery. The little girl made a funeral pyre for the two fish and set fire to it. The fat from the two fish formed a little mound that became bigger and bigger, and then higher and higher, carrying the little girl to the moon. The little girl was adopted by the rain god, and soon was married to the rain god's nephew, the lightning. The girl returned to her village with her husband to pay respect to her parents after marriage. The stepmother attempted to harm the little girl's husband. The wicked trickery was exposed, and the little girl and her husband the lightning returned to their rain cloud. The rain god, on hearing about the wickedness of the stepmother, was furious and sent down thunderbolts, lightning, and rain in torrents.

Notes

1. A number of tales included in this volume published by Sterling Publishers also appear in Maung's other collections, such as *Burmese Folk-Tales*, published by Oxford University Press (India), and *Burmese Law Tales*, published by Oxford University Press (U.K.). To facilitate the analysis and discussion of functional events making up the storyline of a folk tale, those tales, which also appear in the other volumes, are reproduced in this study with the permission of Oxford University Press (India) and Oxford University Press (U.K.). For the rest of the tales, summaries are provided wherever relevant.
2. Narratology primarily denotes the theory and the study of narrative and its structure.
3. This tale is included with the permission of Oxford University Press (India).
4. This tale is included with the permission of Oxford University Press (India).
5. This tale is included with the permission of Oxford University Press (India).
6. This tale is included with the permission of Oxford University Press (U.K.).
7. This tale is included with the permission of Oxford University Press (India).
8. This tale is included with the permission of Oxford University Press (India).
9. This tale is included with the permission of Oxford University Press (India).

REFERENCES

Abbott, G., & Khin T. H. (2000). *The folk tales of Burma: An introduction*. Leiden: Brill.

Abbott, P. H. (2002). *The Cambridge introduction to narrative*. Cambridge; New York: Cambridge University Press.

Alber, J. (2002). The 'moreness' or 'lessness' of 'natural' narratology: Samuel Beckett's 'lessness' reconsidered. *Style*, *36*(1), 54–75.

Bal, M. (1985). *Narratology: Introduction to the theory of narrative* (1st ed.). Toronto: University of Toronto Press.

Bloome, D. (2003). Narrative discourse. In A. C. Graesser, M. A. Gernsbacher, & S. R. Goldman (Eds.), *Handbook of discourse processes* (pp. 287–319). Mahwah, NJ; London: Lawrence Erlbaum Associates.

Bremond, C. (1977). The morphology of the French fairy tale: The ethical model. In H. Jason & D. Segal (Eds.), *Patterns in oral literature* (pp. 49–76). The Hague; Paris: Mouton.

Brewer, W. F., & Lichtenstein, E. H. (1982). Stories are to entertain: A structural-affect theory of stories. *Journal of Pragmatics, 6*, 473–486.

Bunanta, M. (2003). *Indonesian folktales*. M. R. MacDonald (Ed.). Westport, CT: Libraries Unlimited.

Carrison, M. P. (1987). *Cambodian folk stories from the Gatiloke*. Rutland, VT: C. E. Tuttle Co.

Chatman, S. (1978). *Story and discourse: Narrative structure in fiction and film*. Ithaca, NY; London: Cornell University Press.

Dan, I. (1977). The innocent persecuted protagonistine: An attempt at a model for the surface level of the narrative structure of the female fairy tale. In H. Jason & D. Segal (Eds.), *Patterns in oral literature* (pp. 13–30). The Hague; Paris: Mouton.

de Beaugrande, R. (1982). The story of grammars and the grammar of stories. *Journal of Pragmatics*, *6*, 383–422.

Drory, R. (1977). Ali Baba and the forty thieves: An attempt at a model for the narrative structure of the reward-and-punishment fairy tale. In H. Jason & D. Segal (Eds.), *Patterns in oral literature* (pp. 31–48). The Hague; Paris: Mouton.

Dundes, A. (1965). Structural typology in North American Indian folktales. In A. Dundes (Ed.), *The study of folklore* (pp. 206–214). Englewood Cliffs, NJ: Prentice Hall.

Dundes, A. (1971). The making and breaking of friendship as a structural frame in African folk tales. In P. Maranda & E. K. Maranda (Eds.), *Structural analysis of oral tradition* (pp. 171–185). Philadelphia: University of Pennsylvania Press.

Dundes, A. (1980). *Interpreting folklore*. Bloomington: Indiana University Press.

Eugenio, D. L. (Ed.). (1995). *ASEAN folk literature: An anthology*. Manila: ASEAN Committee on Culture and Information.

Fludernik, M. (1996). *Towards a 'natural' narratology*. London: Routledge.

Fludernik, M. (2003). Natural narratology and cognitive parameters. In D. Herman (Ed.), *Narrative theory and the cognitive sciences* (pp. 243–270). Stanford, CA: Center for the Study of Language and Information.

Gabriel, Y. (2000). *Storytelling in organizations: Facts, fictions, and fantasies*. New York: Oxford University Press.

Genette, G. (1980). *Narrative discourse: An essay in method*. Oxford: Basil Blackwell.

Georges, R. A. (1970). Structure in folktales: A generative-transformational approach. *The Conch*, 2(2), 4–17.

Giora, R. (1991). On the cognitive aspects of the jokes. *Journal of Pragmatics*, *16*(5), 465–485.

Grayson, J. H. (2002). The Hungbu and Nolbu tale type: A Korean double contrastive narrative structure. *Folklore*, *113*(1), 51–69.

Güttgemanns, E. (1977). Fundamentals of a grammar of oral literature. In H. Jason & D. Segal (Eds.), *Patterns in oral literature* (pp. 77–97). The Hague; Paris: Mouton.

Hasan, R. (1996). The nursery tales as a genre. In C. Cloran, D. Butt, & G. Williams (Eds.), *Ways of saying: Ways of meaning* (pp. 51–72). London: Cassell.

Herman, D. (2002). *Story logic: Problems and possibilities of narrative*. Lincoln; London: University of Nebraska Press.

Hoey, M. (2001). *Textual interaction: An introduction to written discourse analysis*. London; New York: Routledge.

Horner, G. R. (1970). A structural analysis of Bulu (African) folktales. *The Conch*, *2*(2), 18–28.

Jason, H. (1977). A model for narrative structure in oral literature. In H. Jason & D. Segal (Eds.), *Patterns in oral literature* (pp. 99–139). The Hague; Paris: Mouton.

Jason, H., & Segal, D. (1977). Introduction. In H. Jason & D. Segal (Eds.), *Patterns in oral literature* (pp. 1–10). The Hague; Paris: Mouton.

Johnson, N. S., & Mandler, J. M. (1980). A tale of two structures: Underlying and surface forms in stories. *Poetics*, *9*, 51–86.

Jumsai, M., & Luang, M. (1977). *Thai folk tales: A selection out of gems of Thai literature*. Bangkok: Chalermnit Press.

Kress, G., & van Leeuwen, T. (2001). *Multimodal discourse: The modes and media of contemporary communication*. London: Arnold.

Labov, W. (1972). *Language in the inner city: Studies in the Black English Vernacular*. Philadelphia: University of Pennsylvania Press.

Labov, W., & Waletzky, J. (1967). Narrative analysis: Oral versions of personal experience. In J. Helm (Ed.), *Essays on the verbal and visual arts* (pp. 12–44). Seattle: University of Washington Press.

Leitch, T. M. (1986). *What stories are: Narrative theory and interpretation*. University Park; London: Pennsylvania State University Press.

Lepper, G. (2000). *Categories in text and talk*. London: Sage.

Lim, C., Tan, L., & Wee, N. (2001). *Proppian fairy tale generator.* Retrieved February 2002 from http://www.brown.edu/Courses/FR0133/Fairytale_Generator/gen.html

Lipman, D. (1999). *Improving your storytelling: Beyond the basics for all who tell stories in work or play*. Little Rock, AR: August House.

Livo, N. J., & Reitz, S. A. (1986). *Storytelling: Process and practice*. Littleton, CO: Libraries Unlimited.

Lüthi, M. (1982). *The European folktale: Form and nature*. Philadelphia: Institute for the Study of Human Issues.

MacDonald, M. R. (1982). *The storyteller's sourcebook: A subject, title, and motif index to folklore collections for children* (1st ed.). Detroit, MI: Neal-Schuman Publishers in association with Gale Research Company.

MacDonald, M. R. (1999a). Editor's note. In M. R. MacDonald (Ed.), *Traditional storytelling today: An international sourcebook* (pp. xiii–xiv). Chicago; London: Fitzroy Dearborn.

MacDonald, M. R. (1999b). Fifty functions of storytelling. In M. R. MacDonald (Ed.), *Traditional storytelling today: An international sourcebook* (pp. 408–415). Chicago; London: Fitzroy Dearborn.

MacDonald, M. R. (Ed.). (2008). *The singing top: Tales from Malaysia, Singapore, and Brunei*. Westport, CT: Libraries Unlimited.

Martin, W. (1986). *Recent theories of narrative*. Ithaca, NY; London: Cornell University Press.

Maung, H. A. (1948). *Burmese folk-tales*. London; New York: Oxford University Press.

Maung, H. A. (1962). *Burmese law tales*. London; New York: Oxford University Press.

Maung, H. A. (1966). *Burmese monk's tales*. New York: Columbia University Press.

Maung, H. A. (1976). *Folk tales of Burma*. New Delhi: Sterling.

Miller, E. (1996). Visuals accompanying face-to-face storytelling. MA essay, Gallation School of New York University.

Retrieved January 20, 2005, from http://ccat.sas.upenn.edu/~emiller/MA_essay.html

Ochs, E., & Capps, L. (2001). *Living narrative: Creating lives in everyday storytelling*. Cambridge, MA: Harvard University Press.

Oring, E. (1986). Folk narratives. In E. Oring (Ed.), *Folk groups and folklore genres: An introduction* (pp. 121–145). Logan: Utah State University Press.

Pellowski, A. (1990). *The world of storytelling*. Bronx, NY: The H. W. Wilson Company.

Polkinghorne, D. E. (1991). Narrative and self-concept. *Journal of Narrative and Life History*, *1*, 135–153.

Prince, G. (1997). Narratology and narratological analysis. *Journal of Narrative and Life History*, *7*, 39–44.

Prince, G. (2001). Revisiting narrativity. In B. Nelson, A. Freadman, & P. Anderson (Eds.), *Telling performances: Essays on gender, narrative, and performance* (pp. 27–38). Newark: University of Delaware Press; London: Associated University Press.

Prince, G. (2005). Narrativity. In D. Herman, M. Jahn, & M. Ryan (Eds.), *Routledge encyclopedia of narrative theory* (pp. 387–388). London; New York: Routledge.

Propp, V. (1968). *Morphology of the folktale* (2nd ed.) Austin; London: University of Texas Press.

Propp, V. (1975). The 'function' of the fairy tale. In F. J. Oinas & S. Soudakoff (Eds.), *The study of Russian folklore* (pp. 163–168). The Hague: Mouton.

Rimmon-Kenan, S. (1983). *Narrative fiction* (1st ed.). London; New York: Methuen.

Rimmon-Kenan, S. (2002). *Narrative fiction* (2nd ed.). London; New York: Routledge.

Röhrich, L. (1991). *Folktales and reality*. Bloomington: Indiana University Press.

Rouheir-Willoughby, J. *Propp's structure of the magic tale*. Retrieved February 2002 from http://www.uky.edu/~jrouhie/rae370_proppmagic.html

Ryan, M. (1992). The modes of narrativity and their visual metaphors. *Style*, *26*, 369–387.

Sacks, H. (1992). *Lecture on conversation, Volume 1* (G. Jefferson, Ed.). Oxford: Blackwell.

Sawyer, R. (1976). *The way of the storyteller*. Harmondsworth: Penguin.

Sobol, J. (2008). Contemporary storytelling: Revived tradition art and protean social agent. *Storytelling, Self, Society: An Interdisciplinary Journal of Storytelling Studies*, *4*(2), 122–133.

Stein, N. L. (1982). The definition of a story. *Journal of Pragmatics*, *6*, 487–507.

Swales, J. M. (1990). *Genre analysis: English in academic and research settings*. Cambridge; New York: Cambridge University Press.

Talib, I. S. (2002). *EL 4221: Narrative structures*. Retrieved January 2002 from http://courses.nus.edu.sg/course/ellibst/narr-str.html

Talib, I. S. (2004). *Narrative theory*. Retrieved between 2005 and 2006 from http://courses.nus.edu.sg/course/ellibst/NarrativeTheory/

Taylor, E. K. (2000). *Using folktales*. Cambridge: Cambridge University Press.

Tedlock, D. (1983). *The spoken word and the work of interpretation*. Philadelphia: University of Pennsylvania Press.

Toolan, M. J. (1988). *Narrative: A critical linguistic introduction* (1st ed.). London; New York: Routledge.

Toolan, M. J. (1998). *Language in literature: An introduction to stylistics*. London: Arnold.

Toolan, M. J. (2001). *Narrative: A critical linguistic introduction* (2nd ed.). New York: Routledge.

Tossa, W. (2008). *Lao folktales*. M. R. MacDonald (Ed.). Westport, CT: Libraries Unlimited.

Zipes, J. (Ed.). (2000). *The Oxford companion to fairy tales: The Western fairy tale tradition from Medieval to modern*. New York: Oxford University Press.

Index

www.ingramcontent.com/pod-product-compliance
Lightning Source LLC
Chambersburg PA
CBHW020942310726
48980CB00001B/12
9781604977165